I0671768

Prom Night
in
Purgatory

by

Kacey Mark

Purgatory Series

Prom Night in Purgatory

Cover Art by *Diana Carlile*

The Wild Rose Press, Inc.
PO Box 708
Adams Basin, NY 14410-0708
Visit us at www.thewildrosepress.com

Publishing History
First Black Rose Edition, 2014
Print ISBN 978-1-62830-501-2
Digital ISBN 978-1-62830-502-9

Purgatory Series
Published in the United States of America

Baila nudged her sister.

"What's wrong? What's going on?" She searched Emilia's face for some flicker of direction. She didn't find any. Her sister's eyes were drowning in a hypnotic whirlpool of regret. Her lips barely moved. "There's more. We're outnumbered. And they're coming for us."

A clammy heap of dread dumped over Baila. "Can you open a portal? Send them back?" She pivoted toward the exit, but before the command to flee left her mouth, she sucked it back into her throat.

A churning pillar of black mist pulled apart with claw-like hands to reveal the tall silhouette of a solid man. Milky moonlight poured warmth over broad shoulders and olive skin.

Asher. She'd recognize that arrogant head-tilt anywhere.

Baila swallowed against the lump still caught in her throat and willed herself not to panic. She'd been in tighter spots before. She could handle this guy—and his risen-from-the-bowels-of-hell routine. *No problem.*

The man started toward her. Glacier-gray eyes lit with mischief as his gaze traveled the full length of her body. He thumbed open the first button of his round-collared shirt. "Welcome to purgatory, Ms. Baila."

Her words fused together in panic when his hands moved to undo the second button. "What are you doing?"

The slight twitch of his lips formed the only response.

Oh...crap. She staggered back. Now would be a really good time to call him off, or send him to the light—whatever people did with overeager spirits.

Chapter One

Baila Grey took a deep breath and pushed her bedroom door open. The creak of the hinges stretched through the room and the muscles between her shoulders tightened. The thick aroma of spice candles and school books rushed to meet her, but thankfully, not her mother.

Soon the groan of Principal Grey's office chair would cut through the soft chatter of the eleven o'clock news.

Aaaaany minute now.

Baila moved into the hall with slow, measured steps, careful to avoid the hidden squeak in the floorboards. How stupid was this? At the limber age of twenty-five, she still feared the wrath of her own mother. She sighed. This had to stop.

The deluge of keystrokes from the office continued without pause. Working late again. Pretty common practice for a principal this close to graduation time, but to Baila, it only served as a warning for the misery yet to come.

Three months of summer meant a full ninety days of uninterrupted sympathy ploys. Baila padded down the stairs with her flats clenched tight in her fist. The double pane office doors were wide open. She caught a glimpse of her mother's blood-shot eyes transfixed in the glow of her monitor.

Her mother's brows inched up. "Where you headed?"

Ugh. Baila turned away and dropped her shoes to the floor. Her mother's voice sounded airy and distant. She'd been crying again.

Baila shook her head. *Not tonight.* She couldn't. She slipped into her shoes with one hand braced on the wall. "The girls and I are headed for Saltair."

"The old resort? This late at night?"

Baila paused.

Her mother gave her a doubtful huff, which Baila dismissed. Soon the questions would fly. Anything to stall her hasty exit and buy more time. No, she didn't need any EVP detectors, laser grids, or full spectrum equipment tonight. The ghosts at Saltair had become aggressive enough to make even the most skeptical believe. They weren't being paid to prove their existence. Baila and her team were paid to get rid of them.

Her mother's voice lifted. "Well, I guess your line of work wouldn't be as effective with traditional office hours."

She ignored her mother's acidic tone and gave a reluctant salute over her head. That's right, only ghost busters and prostitutes kept hours like these.

Good thing Baila had an "in" with the other side. She'd make a pitiful prostitute.

"Don't wait up," Baila called.

The groan and pop of the leather office chair signaled her mother's full attention. "But what about your birthday? I had a cake and everything."

Baila's mind chased back to the kitchen where a half-eaten, two-layer carrot cake sat mutilated on the

2

counter. "We did that for lunch, remember?" Four agonizing hours spent with her mother and The Faculty Friends seemed more than enough.

"How long will you be gone?" her mother grunted as she pulled herself from the chair.

"As long as it takes. Saltair's a big place. If you want it safe for the senior prom…"

Her mother's heavy-heeled steps took pause. "Oh, speaking of that. I was wondering—"

"Never a good thing," Baila muttered.

"—what was that?"

She made a reluctant pivot and offered what she hoped was a patient smile.

Her mother tipped her head of mousy-brown locks. She had that crazy-eyed look again. The "misery" look. The one that made Baila want to fire the starting pistol and race for the front door.

"What do you think about chaperoning? You know, in case some straggling ghosts might need attention."

She shifted her purse higher on her shoulder. "We're very thorough."

Her mother splayed her hands in a jazzy, ta-da motion. "I know. The best exterminators in the state. But the parents will want some form of reassurance. Besides, I already picked up a new scarf for the dance. It's on your bed."—she wiggled her fingers—"It's all glittery and…oh, it'll be perfect."

She fought to suppress her instinctive eye-roll. "It's been years, ya know. You seem to keep forgetting I have hair now."

"Don't be silly. Scarves just look pretty on you, that's all. A lot of old friends haven't seen you yet. We should make a good impression."

Baila spun for the door with growing force in each step. "I'll go, but I'm not wearing the scarf."

An all-knowing smile crept into her mother's voice. "Why don't you sleep on it? I'm sure all that energy and excitement for tonight has you feeling a little fired up. We'll talk about it tomorrow."

"Good-bye mother." The front door slapped shut behind her, but the sigh of relief didn't come. Baila marched for the car, burning off the remnants of frustration as she stroked a protective hand over her curls. She knew that tone. Even now, it ate at the edge of her nerves.

Eight years ago, on the first ride home from the cancer clinic, her strength and awareness had been leached by the malice of modern medicine.

Late-afternoon sun had glanced off the house's broad windows and flashed in her face as the car jostled into the driveway. The balmy summer air churned her stomach. Her mother had led her up each stair with a protective arm around her shoulders. "Let's get you to the bathroom," she murmured. "Then you can rest."

Rest. That sounded good. But to curl up and die would've felt better. She sat on the cold bathroom tile with her arms crossed over the porcelain bowl, unable to concentrate on anything apart from her anxious shallow breaths.

No, don't throw up...Don't throw up...Not again.

A clammy tingle had swept over her face.

It was coming.

It sounded like a gunshot went off when her mother snapped on the electric razor. Baila lifted her head when the buzzing sound lowered near her right ear.

"What are you doing?"

Her mother gave that same sad smile and shrugged. "Doctor says it might fall out anyway. We may as well get it over with."

Baila's voice rose in shrill panic. She covered her hair. "I don't want to shave my head!"

"Oh, honey. I know you don't want to, but it'll grow back before you know it. Besides, with all the time you'll be spending in bed, it's too hard to keep the tangles out."

Bile swirled up Baila's throat. She swallowed hard to push it back. "Not now, Mom."

Her mother scowled with one fist planted on her hip. "Yes, now. I know you're a fighter, Baila, but you've got to stop fighting *me*. We've only got each other now. I need you to go with me on this."

Baila's stomach convulsed and she threw up. She could scarcely catch her breath before her body convulsed again. At first she thought it would never stop. Even when her stomach had nothing left to give, still she heaved. But the final blow came when she nearly blacked-out from exhaustion and the cold, metal grit of the buzzer raked against her scalp. Unable to fend her off, or even argue, Baila sobbed as feather-soft waves of hair fell down around her.

Forget the medicine. Her mother had became an even bigger leach. With the week-long parade of friends and acquaintances that followed, she raked in a sizeable profit of attention, and she'd been milking for emotions ever since.

But not anymore.

Baila might be back in town, but things had changed in the last several years. Her determination returned three-fold. Along with her strength—okay, most of her strength.

While she still felt healthy, while she still had the time, Baila would take her life back into her own hands just before she kissed death.

****

They say having one foot in the grave forms a conduit to the afterlife. But as a conduit, Baila never went halfway on anything. She wasn't the kind that would simply dip a toe in to test the water. *Nope.* At the first hint of paranormal intrigue, she jumped with both feet. Never afraid of where she'd land.

Not even her six-month curfew on life could change that.

The growing tingle in her chest kept time with the climbing shaft of light, as it progressed one step at a time, across the balcony of the old pavilion. The place didn't show its age much. Not a single cobwebbed corner. The place looked clean. Perfect. No smudged mirrors or dust bunnies for apparitions to hide in. No drafts or shadows to excuse them away either.

Goosebumps chased up Baila's arms. "How much did you say we're getting paid for this? The place must be positively crawling with energy." Her voice came out louder than expected. The sound echoed off the domed ceiling, down vast hallways, and dashed away from her sister, Emilia, and two best friends.

Emilia gave her younger sister a solute with her plastic champagne glass. "The most haunted place in all of Salt Lake City."

"And most awesome," Baila added.

"Only the best for our birthday girl."

She had that right. Not only did this place offer a

hefty paycheck for their ghost busting services, tonight it would give Baila the best present she could ask for—to not only tempt death, but to get a little action too.

Oh, they'd get rid of the ghosts, all right. All save one. Preferably the hottest one.

Her two friends, Meg and Liz, brushed at the checkered picnic blanket that stretched across the polished dance floor. Liz shook her head. "Extermination or no, holding prom in a place like this is *so* reckless. The Saltair's too close to the gateway."

"Hence the appeal." Meg tipped her head to one side and choppy, calico highlights flipped about her shoulders. "Just think. All those frisky teenagers, a place this remote. This'll be a prom to remember."

Liz shot Meg a long, reproachful look. The two friends were polar opposites. Liz, so constricted she could probably use her bra for a bullwhip, while Meg—well, probably didn't even own one. Neither one was born with paranormal skills, but the extermination team wouldn't be the same without them.

Liz spent her days debunking every paranormal element she could find, and Meg chased them with a torches and pitchforks. It rounded the group out quite nicely.

"You get a bunch of ghosts grinding away on the dance floor, your mom's gonna throw an eppy," Liz said.

Baila smirked at the dim, eight-foot chandelier overhead. "Yes. Yes, I think she will."

Her sister stared. "You're not actually going…"

Baila gave a noncommittal shrug. "She wants a stand-by in case any stray ghosties try crashing the party."

"You should've taken your medicine like the rest of us and gone to your own senior prom. Maybe then she wouldn't push this so hard," Liz said.

"Hey, given the chance, what would you do? Spend senior year traveling the world or groom yourself for the touchy-feely guy in AP English."

Meg held up her hand. "No contest. Bring on the plane ticket."

"Well, at least my prom wasn't held in a death trap." Liz's mouth snapped shut, and a deep blush crept up her neck. Meg and Emilia hit her from both sides with a fierce glare, but Baila pretended not to notice. That kind of don't-let-the-terminal-girl-know-she's-dying scenario went lame a long time ago. The word "death" might be a no-no in this intimate circle of four, but not saying the word wouldn't make it go away. It was inevitable. *Terminal.* May as well embrace it, or in Baila's case, mock it. But to ignore it felt more insulting somehow.

The shaft of pale light arced over the girls as Baila anchored the flashlight to her hip. "I assure you, this place is completely safe. It's only a replica anyway. The original building's remains are still a quarter-mile northwest of here. That's where all the good stuff happens. The replica was moved to avoid the rising water levels." She gave a reluctant nod. "And spirit infestation."

Meg let go a delicate snort. "And how's that going for them?"

"The old place is under water. The replica is close enough…maybe too close. Apparently the ghosts don't know the difference." Emilia cast a suspicious glance around the room in that protective-sister-with-a-splashof-mom expression. "And speaking of open water, there are plenty of *live* fish in the sea, you know. You don't need to go hunting for a dead one. This isn't child's play—like some silly little poltergeist—we're dealing with here. This is serious power."

True. But with sand running low in her hour glass, and Baila's reluctance to land even one steady relationship, she may as well place a few orders with a more permanent crowd. A little unethical maybe, but for one last chance to give death the finger, she needed someone larger than life.

Meg hooked a glob of rose-colored frosting from the edge of the cake and popped it in her mouth. "Baila likes to think big. And let's be honest, the pool doesn't get any bigger than this."

Baila widened her smile, and made a scrunching gesture with her hands. "Ooo. How about a knight? Or a gladiator, that would be fun. All big and muscley and—big."

"Ugh, those dudes didn't bathe. Could you imagine the stench?...Necrotic body odor stew." The serving knife flashed in Meg's hand as she made a coaxing gesture. "Go younger. Cleaner."

Liz frowned as she followed Meg's first slice into the spongy cake. "Seriously, guys, it's not like they're all lined up waiting on the other side."

"And why not? Baila's a great catch. Any boy in school would've killed to go out with her," Emilia said.

Yeah, but that was then. Baila looked to her droopy, chiffon top and loose fitting jeans. She'd regained her strength, but the rounds of chemo thrashed her appetite and whittled her curves down three sizes. When she moved back home, a few guys from her graduating class were still working in family businesses on Main. But with the chime of the entryway bells, announcing her presence, their glances were brief. No recognition lit their eyes. Not that she could blame them, she barely recognized herself.

"So how do you go about choosing one anyway?" Meg asked.

"Easy. Especially in a place this concentrated." Emilia unfolded a wad of photocopies and fanned them out under the languid sway of candle light. "I got these from my old paranormal studies professor, so they're totally legit. Just pick your apparition and I'll do the rest."

The top page framed a hazy image of a man standing at the end of a whitewashed pier. His details looked clouded and wavering, but his posture couldn't be more concrete. His broad shoulders squared against a darkening sky, with hands shoved in his pockets, and his head tipped in challenge.

The perfect adversary against Baila's slow and painful ending. If death was going to take her, damned if she wouldn't at least enjoy the ride.

Meg gave a low whistle. "I might just take a trip down there myself."

Baila lifted her brows in vague agreement. If the guy commanded that much power in ghost form, what had he looked like in the flesh? No, this guy didn't look like he belonged down there at all.

And what is it with people always calling the afterlife "down there" anyway? They'd all seen the gateway. The twin vaulted doors of steel were perched a hundred feet midair. Clearly up, not down.

When the gateways first started to appear, the

government banned them. No one was allowed within half a mile of one. Any person caught jumping the fence would be sucked into the portal.

The twin doors would open... and poof!

Not that anyone really knew for sure. The victims didn't return to verify. Even in spiritual form. But with every disaster that brought mass causalities, another gateway popped up, and it became more difficult to keep the mourners away. As though the heavens decided, with so many people passing through, they may as well build a fashionable entrance. After more than eighty years, the Saltair gateway had become the most feared location in all of Utah.

"You getting something, Emilia?" Baila asked.

Her sister paused. Honey streaked curls swayed as she shook her head.

"Anything would be better than the last time we were all together. Stupid train station. Like *that* was a good idea." Liz wrapped her arms around her cropped cardigan and cast a suspicious frown to the room's darkened corners. "Bunch of grabby-handed hobo ghosties."

Meg gave Liz a look of mock epiphany. "Yeaaah... kind-a like your old prom date huh."

Baila sighed. Bull-Whip Lizzy and Easy-Breezy Meg. Endless hours of joyful bitchery.

"—I was working Baila up to the grand finale," Emilia insisted.

"No, you were *hoping* she'd give up before we got this far," Liz corrected.

True. Baila couldn't really blame the team for their uneasiness. Most of the time, their job meant ridding the world of pesky ghosts that people could *see*. Not conjuring old legends that would just as soon kill you.

Baila toyed with the edge of the photo. "You know me better than that. Just a spoonful of suggestion and I'm going at it like a sailor at port." She held the image at arm's length and gave it a nod. "I like this one."

"Now how did I know you'd pick that one?" Emilia angled her smirk to the massive domed ceiling and closed her eyes. "They call him Gadspy. Legend tells, he hunts the gateway for human souls. He's the one who drags them back there. A real menace, that one." Her voice took on a calming note. "Speaking of menace, you know this place burned down twice?"

Liz pushed a single candle into the first slice of cake and brushed the stray crumbs from the plate. "You mentioned that already. Sounds like this place was never meant to be."

"Well, the ghosts like it. Gadspy's ghost isn't the only one. Countless others have haunted this place over the years. With its proximity to the gateway, it's no wonder this place has become a hub of paranormal activity."

Liz flipped open her lighter and lowered the flame with a steady hand until it licked the tiny pink candle. "You see? That's exactly why nice places like these get all boarded up. People can't afford not to believe in ghost stories anymore."

"Why do they call him Gadspy?" Baila asked. "He must have a real name."

Emilia's voice remained distant. "No one knows who he is. Just that he's young, and looks like he's dressed from the nineteen-twenties."

"What if he's already taken?" Baila asked.

"Won't know till we ask him."

Meg snorted. "You kidding? With that attitude? This boy's far from whipped."

Baila laughed. "Dang. And I left mine at home."

"Trying to concentrate here," Emilia sang out.

Baila pressed her lips together and watched the faint wrinkle play over Emilia's brow. Baila wasn't the communicator, only the conduit. In the paranormal sense, she'd been born with a handicap. Couldn't see. Couldn't hear. But for some reason they just loved to *hang all over her*, like old drunken buddies at the bar.

Her sister had been born with the gift, and polished her skills as a medium and conjurer the summer before she hit college, but dropped everything when one of her classmates turned up dead.

Those that couldn't conjure the departed, or counsel into the light, exterminated. But conjurers weren't easy to come by, they didn't bribe easy. Minor jobs like the train station were easy money for their extermination team, but for a job of this magnitude?

Forget it.

But Baila got lucky with Emilia. She had familial guilt on her side.

She grinned at her sister. "So...would this be like, a long distance call or—"

"Shhh!"

Baila darted a glance around the room. "Why? Is he here?" The bouquet of candles that circled the group didn't extend very far into the room's growing darkness.

"*No, he's not here.*" Emilia frowned and swatted the air near her temple. "Just some old bag lady"—she cringed—"Sorry. *Caretaker* trying to sell me a map of the afterlife."

Baila sat taller. "Well, ask her. Maybe she knows him."

Emilia cracked a glaring eye at Baila before closing it again. She let out a heavy sigh. "Oh—kay, *Mildred*, can you tell me where Gadspy is?"

The room grew still, and Baila's heart sped to a giddy rhythm. "What'd she say?"

Her sister's voice fell flat. "She says, 'who's Gadspy?'"

Baila lifted the picture and faced it to Emilia. "Tell her it's the guy. The hot one who hangs out here."

"Says she hasn't seen him."

"She's lying. She has to be. Maybe we should offer her something. A bribe."

Emilia's eyes popped open. "She can hear you, ya know. Besides, what do I have to offer—"

Emilia tucked back her chin and pushed her diamond necklace down her shirt, as if some unknown voice had just answered her question. "No-ho-way. Do you have any idea how much this cost?"

"Offer her some cake instead. Do ghosts eat cake?"

Meg gave her a flat look. "Do they wear jewelry?"

The girls looked at each other and shrugged.

"All right. Cake then. Do we have a deal? " Baila asked.

Emilia's shoulders set back in triumph. "She says his real name's Asher. And if we want a good look at him we'll have to go out to the pier."

"What pier?"

Emilia paused and shook her head again. "That's all she's giving me. Says we shouldn't have gone cheap on the butter cream frosting." Her shoulders dropped in their sockets. "This isn't going to work. I'm getting

14

nothing here. Baila, give him a shout out. Maybe it'll pique his interest."

Baila gave her sister a long look. "Oh-kay." She pulled in a tight breath and paused. How do you pick up an eighty-plus-year-old ghost when you can't even hack it with the guys your own age? She'd had her fair share of romances in the past, but they didn't last long. And her reputation with the ghost community proved even more fleeting.

Emilia must have sensed her hesitation. The barest hint of a smile curved her lips. "Just call him by name and tell him why you're here. Open your mind and invite them in. Like you always do"—she made a grand gesture with her hand—"and in marches the man-meat parade."

Baila nodded and closed her eyes, but unbeknownst to her girly clan, Baila never did anything special to invite them. They just…showed up. Her conducting skills came with nothing more than a stroke of luck. If you could call it that.

Maybe she should've conducted a practice run before trying to use the mad skills she didn't really have.

Oh well. Bombs away. "So, Gadspy—"

"Asher," Emilia corrected. "If you don't call him by the right name, he's not going to answer."

"Right. Asher. The hot muffin of studliness."

Meg snorted. "Oh, that'll work—"

Baila continued without pause. "I happen to be short a date for the most demeaning event of my life. Ghost patrolling the senior prom. So if you could be a good boy and show yourself, I've got a little present for you." Baila puckered her lips and held silent for a full agonizing minute, then cracked one eye open.

Emilia frowned. "How do you ever get laid?"

"Oh, enough of this. It's almost midnight." Liz straightened. "Time to toast your birthday. Besides, he can't make your wish come true if you haven't even made one." The paper plate bowed under its confectionary burden as Liz lowered a thick wedge of cake into Baila's lap.

She cradled it with both hands. Her chest constricted at the tiny jumping flame and the milky beads of wax pooling at the candle's base.

It's a lame tradition to always blow out the candles first. One that Baila and her friends had always protested. Life was too short, and the most important wishes had a sick way of not coming true. So eat the cake first. Take from life what you will and save the frivolous wishes for later.

But if she did believe in wishes...She wouldn't be wishing for a date.

No. She'd be wishing for more time.

The heavy silence said her friends wanted that too.

She pushed back the tears that pricked behind her eyes and pulled out her biggest smile. She scooped a fork full of cake into her mouth and after a difficult swallow, she steadied her voice. "Kay...I wish—"

"For one big hunk-a-man," Meg blurted out, dabbing at her painted lashes.

A sob surged up Baila's throat, but she pushed it back and tightened her unsteadying grin. "Oh, and not just any man. The most eligible bachelor in the entire afterlife."

Liz waved a hand at her. "Okay, hurry up. The wax is melting,"

Baila took a deep breath and closed her eyes. She leaned forward, but stilled as all the air seemed to suck from the room.

An icy chill wrapped around her shoulders and held her there in a frosted tomb, unable to move forward or back. Her eyes popped open and she pulled in a startled gasp.

The candle flickered out, leaving behind a thin plume of smoke that spiraled into the muggy summer air.

The blanket of ice whipped away from her shoulders.

The semicircle of votive candles around them continued their cheerful sway, completely undisturbed.

Uncertainty needled up Baila's spine and she twisted to the empty space behind her. "Hey! Someone stole my wish."

"I didn't do it." Meg professed.

She turned her frown on her two friends, then to Emilia. "Mildred maybe?"

Her sister shook her head slow, with a frosting coated fork still poised at her lower lip.

Liz pushed her plate away. "Okay now I'm officially freaked."

"Is—is he here?" Baila asked.

"If he is, he's not showing himself," Emilia replied.

Baila didn't need to hear her sister's shaky tone to know that she was spooked. But coming from Emilia, the wavy unease seemed to feed to every person in the room. Including Mildred, who had disappeared just as quickly as she'd come.

Baila raised her voice. "Funny, he doesn't seem like the bashful type."

It probably wasn't the best idea to provoke him, but someone owed her a wish, damn it. And they better pay up.

"I don't think he wants us here," Emilia said.

The chandelier above them quivered, the sound like a chorus of a million fairies crying in terror.

Emilia's voice lowered to an urgent whisper. "I mean it, guys. We've got to go—"

A large moth darted from the pendants of shivering glass above and fluttered toward Emilia. It's fuzzy, white legs braced for landing.

Emilia's body went tense.

Baila waved a hand through the air to deter the bug from its path. "Calm down Em, it's not going to kill you—"

Baila rocked back as a second moth of equal size flew only inches from her face.

"Look! Where are they all coming from?" Meg asked.

Emilia made a full body shiver when her attention fell to another moth dancing in circles on her knee. "Eww god. Get it off. Get it off!"

Baila scooped it into her hand. "They're harmless—"

"They're freaking huge!" Emilia watched the moth with suspicion as Baila tossed it away. "That thing came from somewhere else."

"What are you talking about? From where?"

Emilia shot her a do-I-really-need-to-answer-that kind of look.

A pendant of cut glass slipped free and crashed at their feet, followed by another.

Baila's friends scuttled backward with a collective

shriek and their attention flew to the chandelier.

A dark swarm of moths descended on the unlit fixture above. Countless winged bodies clung to the pendants like tiny bats. And more were collecting from every direction.

Emilia snatched the corners of the blanket. Plates and cups rolled to the center. The cake mashed face-down and frothing champagne spilled over as she lifted the entire bundle into her arms. Her words galloped together. "The hole's too big. I can't close that, it's…it's…We have to go right now."

A low groan stretched across the ceiling. The plaster above the chandelier cracked and branched. A fine powder wafted to the floor.

Those little moth bodies couldn't weigh enough to bring the entire fixture down, could they?

Baila stepped back as a second groan erupted. The fixture jerked. Several moths displaced by the commotion fluttered away on a haphazard course into the darkness.

Without warning, the entire swarm lifted from their perch and spread in every direction, beyond the reach of candle light.

Baila moved for the picnic basket, but a sudden fear raced over her muscles and glued her in place for a second time. A hum of energy stretched up behind her. Something cold, and compelling, and slightly pissed if she wasn't mistaken. The tickle of chalky wings chased up her arms.

Emilia gave Baila an urgent look, then her startled, periwinkle gaze rose higher to the dark force that Baila could feel growing behind her.

Emilia stumbled back. Her mouth opened in a

soundless gasp.

"Don't just stand there," Meg urged. The energy collapsed in a rush of air and scattering wings, when Meg barreled through it to snatch Baila's arm.

Baila ran down the hallway with cold fear and the scamper of her friend's footsteps chasing after her. She hit the front door with both palms, and pushed into the parking lot, but the lukewarm that greeted her couldn't touch the numbness that prickled over her skin. "What was that?"

Emilia looked up from her hunched position and spoke between panicked breaths. "Don't know. I've never seen anything like it. The way they swarmed into a giant mass like that."

Liz's heels hammered the pavement as she marched to the car. "Is this your idea of joke? 'Cause seriously, it's not funny."

Baila marched after her. "You're telling me you didn't see that? Meg walked right through it. How could you not?"

"Knock it off. I'm warning you." Liz lowered her voice to a grumble. "There's a logical explanation. A few boxes of bugs and some fishing line. That's all it would take. You people are ridiculous."

Meg gave an exaggerated eye roll as she chased after Liz. "Would you calm down?"

"You guys know I hate stuff like this," Liz continued, her voice quivering. "And what the hell were you talking about? The hole's too big. It's never too big. We've always sent them back. Always! I don't know why I ever agreed to come out here." She fumbled through her keys with shaking hands until they dropped to the ground.

Emilia's voice took on a gentle hush. "You know why we're out here. This is Baila's final wish."

Liz stooped to pick up the keys, but Baila was faster.

She stared at Baila's open palm, but didn't take the keys. Instead, she clamped a manicured hand over her mouth and pulled Baila into a tight hug. She didn't make a sound, but she didn't have to. The quake of her shoulders said plenty.

Baila managed a gentle pat on the back and fought the urge to melt into a puddle of tears right along with her. "You know what? You're right. This is my deal. Not yours. I shouldn't have dragged you into it."

Liz pulled away with her head down.

Bull-Whip Lizzy, The diva of indifference and the logical solution to all things unexplainable, seemed to shrink under the weight of her own fear. "This job was too big for us. We never should have agreed…"

Baila looked back to the building. The main entry lit with a faint glow from the forgotten candles inside. They wouldn't do much damage on their own. Probably fizzle out in a few hours. But with the growing rage that crawled under Baila's skin, she wished she'd been armed with a flame thrower instead of a flashlight. That stuck-up puff of smoke had no right scaring her friends like that. This was between Baila and Asher. No job would get the better of her. Especially not this one.

"You guys go ahead. There's something I've got to do."

Emilia issued her a stern look. "You're not going back in there. Not alone."

"No." She pulled back and angled her head northwest. "To the pier. Gonna get the bastard where he lives."

Liz dabbed at her nose. "Emilia's right. You're not going alone. But just so you know, you have officially reached a new level of insanity."

Baila grinned."Mmm. And the night's still young."

"Fine. But there's nothing left out there," Emilia said.

Oh, yes, there was. The gateway. Baila hadn't planned to go that far tonight, but when she got pissed she didn't back down.

Her mind flashed to the photo she'd held only minutes ago. That smug angle of his head—she could almost hear him laughing now, a low-slung chuckle that itched around her nerve endings.

That pier had to be around here somewhere. Judging from the photo, probably closer to the gateway where the original building lay buried. And if Gadspy's ghost had been there before, he'd show up again. Baila wasn't polished on paranormal etiquette, but there had to be a reason they chose to show in certain places and not in others. Maybe if she stepped into his office, he'd show his face long enough for her to get a few good punches in.

And it wouldn't take much to lure him either, because the force that chased them from the building hadn't stayed behind.

It followed her.

The further that cold, spindly presence pursued her past the Saltair's property line the more convinced she became. This was the man she'd been looking for. The foreign energy had changed somewhat. Not so much angry, but distant and watchful now. And it didn't belong.

Just like the man in the photo.

She cast a quick glance to her older sister, but Emilia didn't seem to notice the invisible stalker following Baila step for step and strumming fear up and down her spine. She forced herself to breathe against the tension in her ribs.

From the edge of town, they traveled over a wasteland of loose gravel and slabs of fractured cement. Salty summer air came in gusts that stirred the constant haze of mosquitoes. Baila's legs ached with fatigue by the time their destination crept into view.

The skeleton of a rust-eaten railcar marked their destination. The rail used to run from downtown and straight across the lake until it met the Saltair, but now the lone railcar seemed all that remained. The building gone and the gateway standing watch in its place.

Those brave enough to scale the fence had left their mark on the railcar. Cryptic symbols of every shape and color tattooed layer-upon-layer until no single message could be distinguished from another. How many final words had been sprayed on that car? From the sea of paint cans littering the ground, maybe she didn't want to know.

There were rumors of a few that had tempted the gateway and survived. Playing the ultimate game of chicken. There always seemed to be some classmate's brother's friend who had crept out just far enough to feel the gateway's pull and returned with a load in their shorts. "The Pulling Point" they called it. But no *real* person had ever experienced it. Not in Baila's lifetime.

Withering cardboard signs lined the ten-foot, chain link fence with sun-faded messages: "Repent Now," "Be Prepared," and "Look to God First." But the photos, those couldn't be ignored. Dozens of bright smiles reached out to Baila as she passed, some glossy and new, while others bubbled with age. All of them carried the same soundless chant of "Have you seen my child?" The makeshift plots of flowers, and sagging balloons formed a lead weight in her stomach.

What would her mother think if she just disappeared tonight? Hopped the fence and gave herself over to the gateway's magnetic pull. Baila wouldn't want her mother to mourn like these people had. But wouldn't it be easier to avoid the cold hospital bed? The agonizing death? She and her mother spent so much time apart these last few years anyway, and the hurt that brought Baila home was waning fast.

She missed creeping through Mayan ruins in search of wild kings long departed, and floating down the Tarcoles River to seek out haunted tribes. As a ghost whisperer's daughter and divining rod, she'd had an electrifying lifestyle, but since she moved back it wasn't hers anymore.

Baila couldn't keep up with her father's travel schedule, not with all her treatments and medication. His job took him places too remote to sustain her care.

Or that's what he said anyway, but sometimes she wondered if his pretty new assistant didn't help with that decision.

Her parents didn't agree on many things, but they settled this one in record time. Baila would move back home with her mother.

But they overlooked something.

Baila wasn't a child anymore. At twenty-five years old, these were her decisions to make. The adventures wouldn't end for her. She'd find them wherever she could, and keep on taking them until she took her last breath.

Her sister, Emilia stopped cold at the fence line. "You hear something?"

Baila's ears strained to catch the sound of hundreds of fish racing over the water's surface—funny though, no fish could live in the Great Salt Lake. *Too salty…*

She squinted through the silver moonlight spilling over tepid waves, but she couldn't detect anything. Old wooden pilings stretched into the lake like brittle teeth, the only remains of the original building. The gateway's monstrous double doors loomed over the water as a silent slab of black granite.

A low rumble grew at her feet and sent tiny tremors up her legs. The sound of rushing water increased, and the posters trembled against the chain link. Baila squatted to keep from losing her balance. She scanned her surroundings.

Where was the commotion coming from? She squinted at the lake again. The gateway awoke with a pale orange glow that raced around its frame. The double doors cracked apart with a hollow thud and light spilled down on the restless lake.

Meg shrieked in a mix of panic and delight. "Look at that!"

The water churned with thick foam as salt-crusted planks buoyed to the surface under a growing mound of earth. Plank after plank rose to form a rail-lined path that raced from the gateway to the edge of the lake.

The railcar bucked to one side with a groan of metal and teetered on its edge. Baila's breath caught in her throat as she watched the old relic inch closer to toppling until the rails jumped beneath it and the car rocked to the other side with an ear splitting crash.

The planks continued their course unaffected and the chain link fence jumped with a metallic shriek. The path stopped within inches of Baila's toes.

The water rushed forward and Baila and her friends stepped onto the resurrected walkway to escape the bubbling salt water. Cardboard signs and balloons buoyed to the surface, while heavier items sank in the rolling surge.

Baila and her friends exchanged uncertain glances, but before they could choose whether to stay or leave, the rumble quieted to a lingering slosh of water at the shore.

She took several gulps of air before she found her voice. "Interesting. He can raise an entire pier but can't gather enough bones to put in an appearance." She spun to face the menacing presence that continued to stand only inches away.

Meg tipped her head. "Be honest, Baila. You're only interested in one bone." She trotted ahead and lifted the section of torn chain link. "So what are you waiting for?"

Liz's pretty bronze skin blanched white. "You can't go in there! It's against the law. You'll get sucked in."

The foreign presence closed the short distance it had kept from Baila. A chilled breath of sandalwood and leather filtered through the air as she felt the pressure at her back increase. Adrenaline shot through her veins.

A deliberate shove launched her forward two giant steps. Not hard or enough to hurt. More like goading. *Daring her.*

Baila couldn't stop the impish grin. She'd never backed down from a dare.

Emilia seemed to recognize the expression and stepped in front of her with a fighting stance. "This is going too far. You want to mess around with the spirit world, fine. Your nightmares, your problem. So long as you stay with the living. But the moment you cross that fence, you're in their world. There's no telling what could happen."

"What makes you think something's going to happen?" She stared pointedly at her feet and the newly formed pier. "We're already standing in it. What difference does one little fence make?"

Chapter Two

Asher's amulet fed a warm glow through his body the moment the women approached. The thrill of pursuit sprang to life in his veins. He and the amulet became one with a singular overpowering need.

To touch the girl.

It had only been a week since his last excursion, but tonight he wanted this fix. Didn't really want four of them, one would do fine, but the girls wouldn't separate. The young ones always seemed to travel in packs. He could pick off the weak ones that fell behind, but he liked the stronger ones best.

Lilith appreciated them too. Their zest for life made them a powerful commodity, and Lilith enjoyed her power.

As the owner of purgatory's boarding house, Lilith was the only supplier of human aura. Every woman Asher collected became her property the moment he brought her back. With his father looking to retire as ruler over purgatory, Lilith's demands had only increased, but tonight she wouldn't be getting anything. He'd keep this one for himself.

The women slipped through the busted fence one at a time, then Asher fell back in step with the one they called Baila. Such an odd name, really. It didn't define her at all. And those strawberry-blonde curls were an understatement too. She had more fire in her than most women twice her age.

Being a collector meant understanding the female frequency, their 'aura' as most called it, and Baila's appeared stronger than most, which could only mean one thing. She had tapped into him specifically and invited him in.

And who could ignore an invitation like that?

When they reached the threshold of the railcar, they stopped and stared.

He crossed his arms over his chest and followed their gaze. Not an easy feat, even for a collector as powerful as him, but for this many he needed something...elaborate, something to draw them all to the gateway without the chance for escape. The railroad track seemed the perfect solution. Asher was still a gentleman, after all, but he couldn't really throw his coat over a puddle that big.

"We should turn back," Liz said.

Baila slouched. "We've already come this far. I can't just turn around."

But turn around, she did. Asher's pulse thrummed with excitement when she stared right into him—as if she could see him—and her pale brow arced in challenge. In her own way, Baila pushed back. She wanted him to show himself.

"Patience, pretty one," he murmured.

His sly grin snapped off when he caught the sudden tension in Emilia's posture. Damn, forgot about the one with the ears.

Emilia's tone fell flat. "He's here."

"So it would seem," Asher drawled.

"What does he want?" Baila asked.

"What do *I* want?" He thrust his thumb at Baila.

"You dames came looking for me, remember? You called me by name." Not to sound ungrateful. His job came easy when the little gems walked right into his pocket.

"I think he wants to ask us the same question," Emilia said.

All four girls seemed to drop-anchor their nerves and looked anywhere but at him. It wasn't a difficult task. Traveling from the portal's outlet to the gateway and then conjuring an entire half-mile section of railway had depleted his energy. Now he could do little more than hover around with the mosquitoes. If he could get them closer to the gateway, he'd harness the energy to reveal himself. All they had to do was step closer.

Baila shifted her weight from one foot to the other.

"Come on, Baila. Take the bait. It's what you came here for." He nudged her forward again, this time with a quick tap on the ass. She jumped forward and spun around. He couldn't contain his laughter at the look she shot him.

"He knows what you're here for," Emilia said in warning. "And you're right about the attitude."

Baila frowned at her sister. "I guessed that."

Asher leaned close to Emilia's ear. "Hey, big sissy, don't you think it's about time you excused yourself? Baila and I want to get to know each other."

Emilia's cheeks reddened, and an unreadable expression creased her brow.

"What'd he say?" Meg demanded.

She looked to Baila with an apologetic smile. "I don't think you should be left alone with this guy. Sorry. I'm getting a really bad vibe here."

Asher's voice darkened. "Don't forget I still owe her that wish. You invited me here—even introduced us. Least you can do is step aside. Let nature take its course."

Emilia edged away without acknowledging him. "Besides, he says you're not his type."

Asher frowned. "Isn't there some kind of rule against mucking with the translation?"

"—apparently you're too skinny," she continued.

Baila's mouth dropped open in horror.

He took a menacing step toward Emilia. "That's enough out of you—"

Baila's indignation drowned him out. "That's a load of crap, and you know it. If I wasn't his type, he wouldn't have followed us all the way out here."

Emilia's mouth clamped shut.

"He followed us?" Liz demanded.

"—and you didn't even notice, did you?" The cutting words were meant for Emilia, but Baila proved an undeniable point to everyone. No one detected him except Baila because that's the way he wanted it. He wanted her, and he was in control. Not the sister.

And why did that stir such a warmth of excitement in her? He could see it bubbling just under the surface. Most women would be trembling in their miniskirt by now, but this one...she liked it.

"Did he really want us to leave the building, or was that you?" Baila demanded.

Emilia's face went from gentle blush to fire-engine outrage. "He was dropping glass bombs all over the place with his little pet moths. What do you think?"

Baila gave her a long look. "I think I'm tired of you trying to protect me."

Well said. Asher rocked back and looked from one sister to another. His little shower of glass wasn't meant to harm anyone, only scatter them so he could catch Baila. It hadn't gone according to plan, but this outcome proved more entertaining anyway.

It'd be a dandy compromise. If he couldn't take Baila alone, he'd take them all.

When Baila marched into the old railcar with her fists clenched, Asher held back. And after a brief squirm of indecision, the other girls chased after her. One by one they stepped into the old car and crossed the border between their world and his.

Chapter Three

The air grew cold and stale inside the rail car, and wisps of dark energy seemed to stretch blindly through the air.

Liz's harsh tone carried over the residual trickle of water from the pier. "Bails, you're out of your freaking mind."

Baila pivoted around with her face tipped to the railcar's roof. "Hey, Asher, we've come this far, the least you could do is show yourself."

His ears perked to the sound of another male voice. "Yeah, Asher. Surely you're not afraid of a tight little chassis like her."

A frantic hand gesture from Emilia stopped the girls. Her attention shot to where four of Asher's men leered over the railcar's roof.

Gordon, his savvy but somewhat baby-faced assistant, kept imports to purgatory running smooth as silk. If they couldn't import, Harvey, the town's mill foreman and hired muscle, took care of the rest. And then there were the twins. Not so good at obtaining things, but they were scary-good at making things disappear.

Emilia couldn't possibly see any of them. *Yet.* But the chorus of cat calls offered plenty of introductions.

Asher breathed out a snarl of frosty air.

Gordon plopped down on the roof of the car and

dangled his legs over the edge. "That's quite a mixer you've got there, Asher. Need a little help?"

"Got it, thanks."

Emilia jumped away when Asher spoke, but this time he ignored her.

Harvey angled his head to Meg. The cigarette in the corner of his mouth bobbed with each word. "You sure? 'Cause I wouldn't mind helping myself to the flashy little brunette over there."

"This is my find, boys."

A hint of menace crept into Harvey's voice. His eyes narrowed. "Don't kid yourself, Asher. Not even you can handle that many dames at once."

The twins murmured in agreement.

Asher splayed his hands out wide. "And you know how much I love proving you wrong."

With a push of energy from his palms, Asher closed the gap of chain link three hundred yards behind them, sealing the only escape.

The girls spun around with a collective gasp at the metallic screech, but Asher kept his eyes on the men. They could detect the women's life force just as easily as he could. It made them antsy. Unpredictable. If he wasn't careful the entire place could explode into chaos.

"What are you going to do? Bind them all to yourself?" Gordon dangled Lilith's amulet from the crook of his finger. The thick black stone cast tiny flecks of silver as it caught the moon's glow. Every unlucky resident in purgatory owned one, and no two were the same. But only a few carried the power for this job.

Lilith's had power and then some.

"Unless you want a world of trouble on your hands, you better bow out," Gordon said. His voice held that even, courteous tone. The one that made Asher want to put him in a headlock and grind his fist into those glossy, cherub curls.

"I've got a better idea. If you can catch even one of them before I do, you can have them," Asher replied.

"Sounds like my kind of odds." Harvey swung himself over the roof's edge. He landed with what should've been enough power to rumble the entire structure, but being weightless tends to have its advantages when sneaking up on unsuspecting females.

Asher gathered the stale wisps of energy in the air and pulled them to his core. His amulet's warmth increased to a steady burn when his form condensed to a dark mist. The air chilled around him. He took another breath, gathered his strength, and pulled harder. His feet met the ground as the mist compressed further and gravity took hold. The dark cloud lifted from the ground and swirled around him. The steady increase in pressure compacted into bone. Muscles stretched tight and engorged with blood, and skin chased over the surface to complete his human shell.

****

Baila nudged her sister. "What's wrong? What's going on?" She searched Emilia's face for some flicker of direction. She didn't find any. Her sister's eyes were drowning in a hypnotic whirlpool of regret. Her lips barely moved. "There's more. We're outnumbered. And they're coming for us."

A clammy heap of dread dumped over Baila. "Can you open a portal? Send them back?" She pivoted toward the exit, but before the command to flee left her mouth, she sucked it back into her throat.

A churning pillar of black mist pulled apart with claw-like hands to reveal the tall silhouette of a solid man. Milky moonlight poured warmth over broad shoulders and olive skin.

Asher. She'd recognize that arrogant head-tilt anywhere.

Baila swallowed against the lump still caught in her throat and willed herself not to panic. She'd been in tighter spots before. She could handle this guy—and his risen-from-the-bowels-of-hell routine. *No problem.*

The man started toward her. Glacier-gray eyes lit with mischief as his gaze traveled the full length of her body. He thumbed open the first button of his round-collared shirt. "Welcome to purgatory, Ms. Baila."

Her words fused together in panic when his hands moved to undo the second button. "What are you doing?"

The slight twitch of his lips formed the only response.

Oh...crap. She staggered back. Now would be a really good time to call him off, or send him to the light—whatever people did with overeager spirits. But Baila didn't know how. She dove right into this pool of hormonal intrigue without looking. As usual.

She shot a pleading glance to Emilia, "Come on. You're the exterminator."

But Baila wouldn't find any help there. Her sister's focus stuck on the four other columns of smoke that sprang up behind them.

"Bails—" Meg called in warning.

Asher reached into his shirt and retrieved a glossy black medallion. With a swift tug, the chain snapped free. His hand stroked over the long chain as if consoling a treasured pet, and his lips curled to a sly grin.

"Wow, that's...real pretty, but I'm not into jewelry—" The last word squeaked sharp as the chain thickened and expanded in his hand. Its hot yellow glow stretched to the floor and snaked alongside him like a golden whip.

Baila bumped into Emilia's shoulder, then Meg's back as the four of them cinched to a tight circle. She stole a look at the four other men falling into formation. They were surrounded. She clutched Emilia's arm.

"Ah come now, don't be afraid," a man from behind her cooed.

"We don't want to hurt you," said another.

"No, we just want to play a while," chimed twin voices. Their laughter bounded through the open rail car.

Asher silently approached Baila. He swung his arm out wide and cracked his golden whip overhead. The sound lanced through Baila's eardrums and the ringing tone that followed, drowned out her scream. She and her friends cowered for only a second before heeding the instinct to scatter.

Following Liz's escape route, Baila squeezed through a gaping hole in the side of the car.

After racing to a safe distance, Baila's attention veered to the railcar, where Meg had angled her upper body through a busted window.

A large figure rushed her.

"Wait!" Baila screamed.

A brawny, red-haired man caught Meg around the waist as she dropped to the pier. She squirmed and pushed at his thick arms. "Let go!" Her struggle knocked the cigarette from his mouth. Hot embers sparked across the floor and were quickly crushed under the weight of Asher's oxford boot.

With a flick of his wrist, the whip lashed out and wrapped around the brawny assailant's ankle. Asher yanked back on the whip. Both Meg and her captor crashed to the floor.

Asher ripped the man's own amulet from his neck. The man seemed to forget about Meg and lunged for his amulet instead. He missed. And with a stroke of light, his body yanked through the rail car into some invisible portal. Baila blinked then peered closer at the weather-crusted structure that he vanished through, but the torn seam between her world and the next looked undetectable.

The gateway stood only a quarter-mile away. She couldn't see it through the rail car, but she didn't have to. She could feel it. Even the tiny hairs on her arms charged from its magnetic pull.

Asher grabbed Meg's ankle. In mid-crawl, her palms smacked the rough pier as he pulled her back. He whipped out the stolen amulet's long, golden cord and looped it around Meg's feet and arms with inhuman speed as it expanded. When he removed the stone and slipped it into his vest pocket, the cord squeezed tight.

"Let her go!" Baila screamed. She raced forward, hoping to ram Asher with enough force to knock him down—or at least stun him.

He had to know she was headed right for him, but he didn't spare her a glance. Instead, he turned to track the frantic click of Liz's heels as she raced to Meg's side.

Two solid thumps hit the ground behind her as the identical men dropped from the roof of the railcar, but she didn't care. Baila pumped her legs faster. Her feet pounded over soggy wood as she charged after Asher.

Before she made contact, two mirror images rushed from behind her and slammed into his mid-section. The tackle sent all three men crashing to the pier in a cold blast of flying fists and muttered curses.

Asher smashed his elbow into one man's chest. He kicked the other in the face.

Baila stole a short breath of victory before she dropped to Meg's side. Her hands searched over the cord's hot, woven fibers. There had to be a knot there somewhere, but she couldn't find one. As if the rope had meshed itself together without any beginning or end.

Her attention flashed to a cornered Emilia still caught in the railcar and panic shrieked through her brain. They would all be caught if they didn't hurry.

"Liz, help me." Heat seared into Baila's hands as the two girls tried to pry some slack into the cord.

Liz roared in frustration and her knuckles blanched white.

Baila's hands slicked with moisture. "It's not working. Meg, try to wiggle free."

Meg didn't move apart from the slow rise and fall of her chest. Baila pulled back the curtain of calico strands that tumbled over her face. Her eyes were closed. Her features locked like a porcelain doll.

A heavy weight slid into Baila's stomach. No. What had he done? Her gaze flicked to the brawling men only a few feet away.

With the first twin doubled over, Asher snatched

his amulet. Both twins were sucked into the air by some unseen force and vanished through the rail car in another flash of light.

First one man, then two. How many people could those amulets exterminate all at once? And how to get her hands on one?

He rolled to his side and cracked the whip toward Liz. Baila watched her posture stiffen and she collapsed on top of Meg. One arm stretched out tight with the cord wrapped around it. Asher dropped the stolen whip as quickly as he'd used it, without bothering to tie her. He turned for Emilia.

The fear in Baila's veins burned away to anger as she raced Asher across the pier to where Emilia cowered like a frightened kitten. Her wide-eyed panic fixed on a tender-faced stranger and his soothing murmurs. The hush between them seemed almost intimate. He lifted the amulet over his mass of blonde curls and poised it over Emilia.

She dipped her head as if to accept her fate.

Asher struck again with the whip. The well-placed blow ripped the amulet from the stranger's hands. A look of profound surprise crossed the man's angelic features and he flashed away the moment the amulet left his reach.

Asher's movements seemed reflexive as he flicked out the last pilfered amulet and swung its whip over his head.

"No!" Baila slammed into his concrete chest. She staggered back just as the whip wrapped itself around Emilia's neck. Her periwinkle eyes glassed over to a blank stare and her lids closed. Emilia's hands slipped away from the cord, and she crumpled to the floor.

Pain shot through Baila's fist when it cracked against Asher's jaw, but she didn't stop swinging. Asher managed to deflect a few hits with his forearms, then caught both her hands behind her back and her chest pinned against him. She twisted at the steel bands that held her wrists.

"Let them go," she said.

His voice flowed over her like dark molasses. "Now why would I do that?" He moved to bind her wrists with just one hand.

Baila jerked and twisted.

His hold on her slipped. He readjusted, gripped her tighter, and a grin curled his lips. "Feisty."

He hadn't used the whip on her yet. Not with both hands occupied. But he didn't seem to mind the inconvenience.

"This has nothing to do with them."

He lifted one shoulder in a shrug. "They're a bonus. Nothing personal." He tipped his head to one side. "But you and I have a different check to cash, don't we." His lips crushed against hers in a swift and demanding kiss. His frozen lips warmed against her in a rush of heat, and his tongue thrust out to plunder her mouth with alarming force.

At first, Baila couldn't react. The sudden flash in temperature pulled her mind into an undercurrent of panic. Her own weak-kneed response became an even bigger threat than the ghost she clung to. Only he wasn't a ghost. Couldn't be. Since when had ghosts ever felt this strong…this warm…this alive?

She angled her head to take in more of him, curious to taste the foreign power he fed her. He nurtured her budding interest with a groan of approval. A sound that rumbled against her chest and sprung warning signs from every corner of Baila's brain.

The bands around her wrists slipped away when one hand lifted to cradle the base of her neck. The other, holding the amulet, wrapped around her waist.

Baila leaned into him and her hand made a painfully slow descent to cover his. If she could just get her hands on that amulet. It got rid of the others, maybe it would get rid of him too…the moment her fingertips brushed the heated metal she yanked the amulet and cord away.

He pulled back. His glacial eyes narrowed in anger.

Before she could reach his cheek with her flying open palm, he sliced through the air and disappeared.

She gaped in shock, as Liz, Meg, and then Emilia sucked away behind him.

Before Baila could take even one step to follow, the pier beneath her gave way. It didn't collapse—just vanished!

Her stomach clenched as she flailed through open air, desperate for something—anything to grab onto. Her right side slammed into the water's surface and murky salt water rushed over her head.

Time drifted in slow motion through the cloudy lagoon as Baila sank under the force of her fall. The back of her head thumped the jagged lake bottom. Shoulders scraped against rock. Her lungs ached to expand but she fought against it. When her heels met the ground, she planted them and pushed.

She kicked only a short distance before she broke the surface of the water. Her first intake became a panicked air and water mix. Baila coughed and gagged at the brine that flooded her mouth. She scrubbed at her burning eyes and squinted at her surroundings.

The railway was gone. Her friends, gone. Baila bobbed among the tepid, black waves, alone and empty in a graveyard of sun-bleached pilings.

Chapter Four

Water squished between her toes with every step up the walkway. Her path dotted by the amber glow of plastic garden lights haloed with tiny insects. Her mother's vanilla, bungalow-style home nestled under massive oak trees, in the midst of wholesome family living. But the American dream ended the moment she stepped past the white picket fence.

The blue flicker of the television lit the den through lightweight sheers like a silent beacon calling her home. It used to be her father's beacon until his first affair, followed by the second. Her mother said the background noise helped her concentrate, but in truth, she couldn't stand being alone.

Since the day Emilia left for college, her mother's two Xanax and four phone calls a day were dumped in Baila's lap. And when Baila's cancer returned, her mother threw out the grappling hooks. At the time, Baila didn't bother arguing about her mother's motive. How could she? At least someone wanted her around. When her father passed her off for his thrill-seeking lifestyle, Baila had raced home like a whipped puppy— and regretted it ever since.

Baila took another step and froze when the floodlights kicked on, caught somewhere between the instinct to run, and having no place left to go. A feeling Baila should have outgrown years ago.

But after tonight how could she go back in there? How could she pretend that nothing happened? Her mother would ask questions. Hover on every detail. And Baila couldn't lie to save her life. Tonight's tango with Asher—the whip slinger and his wicked tongue proved that. She liked the taste of his control, and she wasn't shy about letting him know it. Trying to steal some of that control for herself had come at a steep price.

Tonight her life twisted into something cold and dirty. Her own selfish expectations pulled her friends and her sister into danger. Their dedication kept them there. And together, the combination destroyed everything. How could she be so stupid?

Baila squeezed the cold amulet in her palm. He took her friends. It should've been her, not them, and she let it happen. She should've fought him every step, but didn't. Trying to win their freedom by kissing him back has been a huge mistake.

Baila took a deep breath and turned the doorknob. The soft chatter of the eleven o'clock news continued without pause, as did the deluge of keystrokes from her mother's adjacent office.

Baila turned away and jerked off her sopping shoes. "I'm home."

"Hey, how was your night?"

Don't respond. If she could beat the hall monitor to the staircase she could avoid more questions.

"I thought you were going to stay at Emilia's tonight," she prompted.

"Change of plans." Baila tried to normalize her soggy gait as she passed the office.

The groan and pop of the leather office chair shot

apprehension up her spine.

"So, what's the status of the Saltair? You think it's prom-worthy," her mother asked.

"Not really."

Principal Grey's voice lifted with interest. "Is that a biased opinion, Baila Jean?"

Baila didn't spare her mother a glance as she rounded the banister and began her quick march up the stairs. "A professional one."

"I'll be sure to consider it then."

"Sure you will," Baila muttered.

"Baila!"

She paused.

"You're completely soaked. And you smell just awful. Like rotten eggs."

"It's a dirty job, mom." She continued up the remaining steps. And it was far from over.

Her mind spun back to the amulet coiled in her palm. Her friends—her real friends never treated her like an invalid. She had always been a person, not a pawn. But to get them back, she would have to become just that.

But how would she conjure Asher again? Baila wasn't even sure how she'd brought him up the first time. And once she managed to get him here, how would she get her friends?

****

Emilia's old room had been converted to a reading area for Baila's personal use, but traces of her sister still lingered. Like the lavender upholstered window seat with its floppy, worn pillows. And the dozens of books still perched on the built-in shelves.

The applied technologies center offered paranormal

studies classes for juniors and seniors. After Toffee, her pet rabbit, died, Emilia had taken them all. Baila wasn't sure what scared her sister away from pursuing her master's in the craft.

Probably a man.

A bitter taste formed at the back of Baila's throat. Her memory flashed to the last moments on the pier, and the way Emilia seemed to bow down. To accept her fate amid the intimate, hushed conversation. It wasn't right. Emilia wouldn't sway so easily.

Her sister had real potential. The skill that would take her far beyond the extermination business and into conjuring—maybe even cross-over counseling. That's where the money was. It took a week's worth of bargaining just to get her out there tonight—that close to the portal.

Could those buried fears be greeting her now? Or even killing her?

The image of Emilia's stricken face flashed through Baila's mind. Her heart squeezed with dread.

No. She jerked the lumpy ottoman under the bookcase and climbed up. She couldn't let fear of the unknown shrivel her determination. Weakness wasn't an option. Not now, not ever. What she needed was a solution.

The four wide volumes angled on the top shelf, were coated with a sticky layer of dust, and the once bright page markers were bent over and yellowed with age. She couldn't go through all of them. No time. Besides, Baila had the attention span of a gnat.

But maybe after skimming over the highlights and adding some online research, she could kludge a decent plan.

Back in her room, she scanned the first table of contents and snapped the book shut. She moved to the next one.

Asher's creepy game of hide-and-seek would be the first to go.

She glanced at the next book's cover, tossed it aside, then held the fourth one at arm's length.

How much of Emilia's "gift" could be learned by the ungifted—the paranormal handicapped? If she could turn herself into a little specter detector, like Emilia, he wouldn't be able to sneak up on her. She might have a fighting chance. He'd already shown himself once. She'd stolen his weapon of choice. The only thing left was to make him an offer he couldn't refuse—whatever the hell that might be.

It seemed a pretty lame trade, three perfectly healthy girls for one sick one. She could only hope the amulet would help tip the scale. He hadn't looked pleased when he'd lost it. The glare of livid surprise, even now, formed a giddy rhythm in Baila's chest.

The bastard.

If he did make the trade, he'd be making that face a lot. She wouldn't make life—or death—easy on him. He might even be tempted to kick her out of purgatory.

After two hours of skimming material in the dim warmth of her room, the flat, black print started to grow fuzzy. The effect on her mind wasn't far behind. She jerked awake when the book slid from her lap and cart wheeled across the shag rug.

For several minutes, she could only stare at it. If she didn't get some rest, her brain wouldn't be any use at all, but she couldn't give up without some kind of progress.

She crawled on heavy limbs from the warm indent on her bed, and lifted the book where its pages mashed against the floor. A glossy photo caught the desk light as it sailed from the book's protective layers and landed face up at her feet.

A tender smile pulled at her lips. Toffee. Her pet rabbit, stretched across the grass with his eyes closed in a blissful sun-bather's grin. His head nestled atop thick sausage rolls of fur. She traced the photo, along the patch of white that dappled his forehead. The same spot he'd use to nudge her hand for attention—would probably nudge the picture right out of it. If he were here.

At ten years old the vet had declared he'd died from natural causes. "A blessing really, for an old bunny to go so fast."

"That's just his way," Baila had sobbed. Toffee never slowed down. Even for the expected Geezer-bunny speed bumps, like his progressive blindness or the sudden aversion for using his litter box.

She knew she shouldn't have asked Emilia to bring him back. But she didn't care.

"He's happier there," Emilia had insisted.

"In the ground? The dirt?" she'd cried.

She'd always asked too much of her sister. Even when Emilia had finally escaped their mother's needy clutches, Baila pulled her back in.

She tucked the picture into the book's binding and scanned the chapter heading.

"To commune with the dead requires nothing more than an open mind, an eager spirit, and a name."

The same line Emilia fed her all those years ago. There wasn't a critter in existence more eager than

Toffee. The problem didn't come from him. It lay in Baila's mind. And that mind was going to open, damn it, if she had to pry it with her bare hands.

She pulled the amulet from her pocket, and slipped the chain over her head. The moment the cold metal slithered between her breasts she felt its warmth begin to spread. The neon green flecks of light stretched and melded together to form a muted glow. The amulet's heat arced panic over her nerve endings.

Maybe this wasn't the best idea. She'd seen how Asher used it. She could wind up gift-wrapped in the corner with a little green come-get-me blinkie light. Kind of hard to strike a bargain from that position.

She listened to the steady hum of insects outside her window. Had the amulet alerted him the moment she put it on? Like some otherworldly GPS? She closed her hand around the amulet, ready to tear it free at the first hint of trouble.

She shut her eyes. "Come on, I can do this. It's not so hard. Just open...open." She tried to balance her breathing and scale her mind's enormous blockade of doubt. She pictured the warmth of the amulet flowing through her, opening doors and shuttered windows. Seeping through brick and melting away walls until only a bare frame remained. Then she mentally whispered Toffee's name, and the old command that always brought him out of hiding.

Peek-a-boo... Peek-a-boo, Toffee...

A heavy weight bounded onto her stomach, and her heart leapt to her throat.

With a sharp gasp, she jackknifed upright.

Something thumped to the ground beside her and scurried across the room. Its claws popped and tore at the carpet in its haste. Baila shot to her knees and flicked a hasty glance around the room. The racing shadow lapped once around the floor, then straight under her bed. Where it *clanged* into the metal bedpost.

Asher wasn't that small. It couldn't be him. And he wasn't the scampering type.

Fear and excitement spun circles inside her, but she couldn't pull her pet's name from her throat. It caught there, snared like a minnow and fighting to free itself. What if she was wrong and had made a terrible mistake? She'd read *The Monkey's Paw*. What if Toffee had come back as some kind of zombie rodent with a taste for human flesh?

Tiny hairs rose on the back of her neck and the amulet glowed brighter. She lowered her upper body over the edge of the bed, but just before her eyes could adjust through the mini landfill of old shoes and magazines, it rushed forward. She shrieked when it flew through her curtain of hair.

The sound seemed to only spur its erratic cut and weave pattern across the floor, until it finally dove into a pile of dirty clothes. Baila kept her eyes fixed on the laundry beast as she reached for something—anything to defend herself. Her first attempt knocked over the table lamp that clattered into a bowl of multicolored spheres. Her mom's voice called out as they pelted the floor.

"Baila?"

"I'm fine!"

She caught the hanger that dangled from her headboard and tore the new scarf away. With one arm wrapped around the bedpost, she stretched forward to prod the pile with a trembling hanger.

51

Nothing.

She swallowed the cold lump forming in her throat and fished the clothes away one item at a time. A patch of tawny fur peeked from under her cut-off shorts. A velvet foot from her twill bucket hat. But seeing his chunky, little tail melted the fear from her bones. This wasn't some emaciated monster, it was her old friend.

Her sister really did it. She had conjured Toffee back from bunny heaven, and he'd raced around unnoticed for years. To everyone except Emilia.

She prodded him with the hanger again and he flinched.

With a deep breath, her racing heart eased. She sat back on her heels and clicked her tongue at him. "Peek-a-boo."

The remainder of the laundry pile flowed to one side as Toffee bounded out. He sprang for the bed, but his lower half dragged behind. Baila lifted his pumping back legs to the heavy chenille blanket. Ashy fur and stiff claws gave way to thin air with only the barest touch. But if her hand hovered in just the right place, the air came to life underneath her. She could touch him...feel him. Her eyes pricked with tears. "Hey, Buddy. How long you been hanging around here?" She stroked the length of his droopy ears. "I wonder how many times I've tripped over you."

Toffee leaned forward to inspect the green glow radiating through the thin ruffles of her shirt. He pushed out an indignant sniff.

Her mind chased back to Asher and the smell of iced sandalwood. She bit back a laugh. "You never did like guys, did you?"

Unfortunately for Toffee, she'd have to make time

for this one. Whether she wanted to or not.

If she could find a crash course to obtain Emilia's skills, she could not only see Asher, but conjure him back at will.

Emilia had pulled him from the ruins of the old Saltair, so why couldn't Baila pull him to her bedroom? She paused. No. Bad idea. After a kiss like that, her bed was the last place she wanted him. She'd given him a day pass to frisky-land when she invited him out the first time. Perpetuating it would only get her in more trouble. Who knows what she'd lose if it happened again?

No. The safest way to fight Asher was to meet him on his own turf.

Chapter Five

Ah, the sting of rejection.

Cold air sand-blasted Asher's skin as his body shot through the portal. His eyes teared and his chest muscles tensed at the frigid pressure as it sucked the air from his lungs.

Double-crossed. By a woman of all things.

The earth and starless sky blurred together. His body tipped and spun. He had to find his bearing fast, otherwise he'd hit the portal's exit like a bug on a windshield. Asher tucked his chin and pinned his arms to his sides. The blur around him grew and his speed increased until a single pinpoint of light mapped his direction. Asher lowered his head just as the light yawned into the first hint of the glossy gray barrier. He gritted his teeth.

That little tease would pay for this.

His body punched through the barrier with a deafening bang that threatened to split his scalp. The air thickened around him and pulled from every angle. His forward momentum slowed to a crawl. Asher somersaulted through the air then landed in a crouch. Hands and feet pounded into the soft grains of a brown sugar beach and scattered a mass of panicked moths.

The rush of blood in his ears calmed to the sound of crying gulls that dipped and soared above him in an everlasting tangerine sky. Carousel music and kettle corn wafted from the old Saltair about a half-mile south. From here, the building and small town that surrounded it, appeared as it should.

A gaudy flea circus of artificial life.

It wouldn't get better up close either. This was home in all its painted on misery.

The adrenaline washed away and cut the fuel supply to his racing pulse. He dipped his head and blew out a heavy sigh. He normally enjoyed the ride, but not when shoved into it head first. Not when it resulted in the loss of his prize. And of course, the added burden of losing the amulet. Without it, his freedom and privilege would dry up. He wouldn't be able to collect the life-sustaining aura from just anyone. He'd be forced to take his daily ration from one of Lilith's caged dolls instead of the free-range fun he'd grown accustomed to.

Speaking of dolls...

He turned back for the portal's outlet. It sucked at his skin and tugged on his legs as he fought his way through the glossy film and back to the frigid blast of air.

The girls weren't dead yet, but with no amulet to grant them passage, they'd never get in alive. If the impact didn't kill them, the repeaters—vagrant, mindless spirits that roamed the outskirts of town, would. He staggered free from the barrier just as the first human parcel came whistling at him. Meg's limp body hit his diaphragm with grand-slam force. The air blasted from his lungs. She slipped down his body to the ground, and he fought for air against the spasms in his chest.

Best job in the world, right? Best job in the world.

The second woman came in higher and faster,

flipping end over end from an awkward angle. He pushed out a growl of irritation.

When he crouched low then sprang to catch her, her shoulder crashed into his sternum and knocked him backward. The barrier squealed a rubbery protest, and flung him forward again. He staggered but managed to maintain his footing. He found just enough time to drop the girl, before the third one hurled straight at him.

He could catch this one more easily, but the trailing cord still dangling from her neck posed another problem. It lashed back and forth along the width of the portal like animated razor wire. Sparks cast from either side where it scraped along the walls.

The moment she hit his chest, he jumped and spread his feet apart taking special care to shield his favorite appendage. The cord lashed between his legs and cracked against the barrier, but not before slicing a gouge into his inner thigh. With a roar of pain, he let the girl slump to the floor and framed the searing wound with both hands.

From the tear in his slacks, he could already see the meaty wound pulling itself together. Muscle reached out from either side. The wound squeezed tiny droplets of blood as the ragged edges fused together. In a moment, the wound had closed and blanched from red to pink. In four seconds flat, his skin smoothed over again. The tear and stanched blood on his slacks the only evidence. After a change of clothes, even that would be gone. Like so many other distant memories that he would never get back.

He shook his head. Masochism ran rampant down here, but it wasn't his thing. Still, in times like these he wouldn't mind a little chronic something to remind him of how it felt to be alive. A tale of too many years in the brickyard or an old football injury—something he could cling to. But like everything else, this injury, this whole day would grow cold and gray for him and eventually disappear.

Baila could've kept him warm for a while with all that pent up energy, but he'd lost her, lost the amulet, and now this. A handful of pretty little burdens and none of them his. Anger rumbled low in his chest. So much for overachievement. He snapped one of the amulets to the chain around Meg's waist and tucked it inside the waistband of her jeans to avoid its contact before throwing her over his shoulder. When he shoved through the portal, the amulet warmed to neon green through the denim. It hissed against her skin and the smell of seared flesh spiraled in his nostrils.

Meg's eyelids cinched tight, but they didn't open. Not until he lowered her to the sand and the amulet's glow faded. The thick chain shrunk to its rested form.

Asher caught the slight flutter of her lashes, and the dawning confusion that furrowed her brow. The sexiest part of the job was watching them wake up, each one an intimate play of emotion that only he got to witness.

Except this time the rush of empowerment didn't come. He looked down. Not even the faintest penile nod of approval. He'd been stiff as a redwood with Baila, but watching Meg gave him nothing. Brilliant. Not only had Baila stolen his amulet, she'd tainted the one pleasure he had left.

He stormed back to the portal again and rammed his shoulder through. When he got a hold of that girl— and he would—he'd give himself a special treat. No sweet dreams for her. He'd drag her down here one hundred percent aware, just to see the panic flare in those feisty blue eyes.

Asher made two more trips through the portal until all three girls sat dazed and speechless at his feet. He turned to the sister. "Emilia, right?"

She drew her knees to her chest. One hand cupped the nape of her neck where the amulet had branded her with the geometric marquis design. She flinched away when he collected the slumbering pendant that had dropped beside her.

"Tell me about your sister," he prompted.

Her voice trembled around the edges. "What did you do with her?"

He frowned. *Not nearly enough.* "Nothing to worry about. Not my type, remember? She's too..." He tapped his lower lip in thought. "Limber, or something." He paused. "No, that wasn't it. I have a great appreciation for flexibility. And with legs like hers?" He gave a low whistle. "Good times. Good times...But we're getting off the subject." Asher snapped his fingers at the coiled chain at her feet. It jumped for Emilia's neck and snaked itself around.

The muscles in her throat worked up and down when she tried to swallow against the constricting cord. Her eyes widened. The bones in her hands stood like talons as she tried to claw her way free.

"Stop. Please," Liz cried from behind her.

Asher shot her a warning look, then turned back to Emilia. He kept his voice calm. Patient. "Where does she live?"

Emilia's words came in a panicked rasp. "On East Side, near Eagle's Grove."

"Stop! You're hurting her." Meg got to her feet,

but was brought down quick by the rapid climb of a second cord. It snaked up her body in a split second, then she too lay gasping for air.

"She live alone?" he continued.

When Emilia flashed a helpless glance to the other girls, he shifted to block her view. Her face grew blistering red. Her mouth opened in a soundless gag.

"Boyfriend?" he asked.

Anger flashed in her eyes, and her jaw snapped shut.

Ah, that would be a no. His chest bounced in a silent snort. He figured she probably strung the last boyfriend up by his testicles. Or maybe he'd cheated on her, and she used her birthday séance as a desperate plot for revenge. Apparently, neither of those was the case.

Baila must've been pretty surprised when he took her up on that offer to appear, but now that she extended it, she wouldn't get it back.

At the first press of Baila's subtle curves, he knew he wanted every ounce of her. Around him, under him, he wasn't picky. Time wasn't much of an issue in his world, and with as lively as Baila felt against him, he'd be sure to hit every angle before he finished with her.

Asher wasn't much for subtlety. Formalities either. He wanted her, he let her know. And...well...now she knew. But it seemed that he and Baila had suffered a little misunderstanding.

There was a name for the kind of girl who reneged on promises like those, who cut and ran at the first sign of intrigue. He wasn't the chasing type, but he sure as hell wouldn't let her best him either. One chance to redeem herself, that's all she'd get. And the perfect opportunity would be coming any day now.

"So, when is this prom you mentioned?" he asked.

Emila's gaze scurried back and forth along the sand as if searching for any excuse to evade him.

He leaned down and pulled the word out slow. "When?"

She squeaked against the gripping cord.

He turned to the other girls. "Anyone?"

The rhythmic shift of sand sounded behind him. Asher threw his senses into high alert. He swiped the remaining cord from the ground and stroked along the chain until it blossomed its full length. The whimper that passed Liz's lips cut short when he pressed a finger to his lips.

The transient repeaters lurking around the city were harmless to its residents, but something about living flesh always drew their curiosity. Every departed soul that first entered purgatory, came with an amulet. A formidable tool for collecting living essence and sustaining a shred of their old life. The repeaters had been stripped of theirs. And their minds had gone with it. They couldn't detect a human's energy level or their body heat, but their sense of smell made up for it. With this many females in close proximity, he'd be a fool not to anticipate them.

"Asher. Asher, old sport, what'd you bring me?"

His shoulders eased their tension. "You? Nothing." He didn't have to turn to recognize the gatekeeper's lanky frame or the crisp fedora bobbing up the sand hill like a dopey giraffe in men's clothing, poised, eloquent…a prize-winning jackass among men.

Elliott's toothy grin stretched wide. "You've got quite a load. And all by yourself?"

"Don't act so surprised."

"Surprised? I'm delighted." He lifted Liz's wrist. "Welcome to purgatory, my dears." Liz tried to pull away before the man's lips made contact, but Asher knew she'd be no match for him. She yelped in fear, but the man didn't seem to notice. His attention snagged on the ornate, pear-shaped brand that blistered white on her forearm.

"What is this? Whose brand is this?" he demanded.

Asher scratched his head. "Gee, I don't know. Not yours, is it?"

His brows shot up from the round, wire frames. "I should hope not. Heads could roll for something like this. Do you have any idea what you've done? How will you explain this?" He lifted her arm to face Asher. "It's not even the right shape. The pattern's completely off."

"You really think I'd attempt a stunt like this without authorization? With everything else I've got on the line?"

Elliott bowed over Liz's arm. "You? Yes."

He grimaced and nodded to himself. "Yeah...Guess you're probably right." With a flash of Asher's hand, all three cords melted back to their original size and dropped to the sand. "But it's my job, my business."

Elliott elevated his voice as the two women lay coughing on the ground.

"True. But what you bring down here affects all of us. Can't have any sicklings passing through. You know what they say, spoils the whole bunch." Elliott closed his eyes. His nostrils flared with a deep intake of breath.

"They look sick to you?"

"You never can tell." When Elliott's lips touched Liz's skin, his moth gray complexion warmed to a dusky peach, as if siphoning the very color from her body.

"Well?" Asher prompted again.

Elliott didn't respond. Too busy suckling his new toy.

Liz's mouth dropped open, and a flash of pain rippled across her brow. "Let go!" Elliott's grip tightened with both hands as she tugged against him. She threw Asher a frantic look.

"Stop leaching my merchandise."Asher smacked the man upside the head with his open palm. Elliott's hat flew through the air and bounced along the beach until it rolled into milky blue water.

Liz shook her hand, then looked to where a pale splotch marred her skin. Frost marks, they called them.

What did she expect? Give a guy like Elliott Deville an opportunity, he'd take it. A lesson these girls had to catch quick if they wanted to survive here.

Elliott squatted down, careful not to touch the lapping water. The hat spun on its top in wobbly circles just beyond his fingertips. "That was new. A gift."

"I'll buy you another."

He dealt Asher a heated glare. "You'll buy more than that. You still owe me for the car you wrecked. I'd be safer taking your cut from Lilith instead. Otherwise I'll never get paid."

Asher shrugged. "Suit yourself. But I wouldn't expect a cut anytime soon."

Elliott stood to his full height. "What do you mean? As soon as you deliver these to Lilith—"

"Nope." Asher tugged the last girl to her feet.

"Let's move."

"Now hang on." Elliott danced ahead of him with his dopey long-legged trot. "I've been mighty tolerant of your unsavory urges until now, but three women at once is more than any man can overlook."

Asher prodded at Meg's back. She shot him a dirty look before shuffling forward.

"Unsavory urges?" Asher mused. "Funny words coming from a man like you."

Elliott straightened. "Beg your pardon?"

He flung the man a passing grin. "Nothing like a nightly spit and polish from your shoeshine boy, right?"

His cheeks darkened. "What I do in my home is my own business."

"Likewise, Elliott." He prodded Meg again, but this time she spun to face him.

"Touch me again, and I will hurt you."

"Sure you will." Asher gathered the free-flowing energy around him, and with an upward scoop of his hand, the women lifted five feet off the ground. Emilia and Liz both gasped and stretched their toes for the ground, while Meg sat Indian style with her chin notched up.

Elliott marched up the sand hill with fists pumping to keep pace with the air-born caravan. "Your father wouldn't like this."

"He can speak for himself."

"That so? Seems to me Ms. Lilith's the one doing all the talking, and I doubt she'd like this at all."

"I think I can handle my own mother." With a quick jab from Asher's elbow, Elliott tumbled down the hill with arms and legs flailing. When he landed, sand sprayed in every direction.

Asher bit back a laugh at the muttered curses and sound of brushing cloth.

"Shouldn't you at least take them for conditioning?" Elliott called.

"They're perfectly conditioned for me." With Meg's sass and Emilia's snappy mouth, they'd put up a fight to remember. And what could be more amusing than that?

****

The Grand Saltair's dining room greeted him with endless tables draped in iridescent cloth and glinting crystal place settings. To the right, twelve end-to-end tables stretched the length of the room with a succulent-looking yet bland-as-all-hell buffet. Citrus fruit wedges heaped over glass bowls. Glazed ham and turkey platters lay interspersed with breads, cheeses, and chocolate. Not a morsel out of place.

Not a good sign.

Asher slowed his pace and peered through the cigarette haze to the deeper end of the room, where four men hunched over the bar's polished surface. "Charlie, Clyde, ready the third floor master suite. We've got company."

The twins spun to face him with double-barrel glares. Like Asher, their injuries had healed, but their egos—not so much.

When he tossed their amulet, both men popped up from their chairs. The scrape of wood overpowered the distant bustle of kitchen pans. Clyde shoulder-bumped his brother from the amulet's path and snatched it from midair. With a grin of victory and a hasty jerk, he pulled the necklace over his head and tucked it inside his shirt. Charlie glowered at him and a charge of cold energy cracked through the room.

Asher continued past them without a glance. Whatever fault they had with each other, they'd settle later. Boredom brings about strange concepts for entertainment in a place like this. Probably why one of their amulets had gone missing in the first place. People enjoyed watching the twins fight over things, but these men weren't the dancing monkey type. Too much pride for that.

They'd rather turn on the nearest friend or enemy and take out their aggression together than to fight in public. That's what Asher liked about them. They always knew how to channel their anger.

Meg looked to Harvey with an emphatic eye-roll. "Oh, great. You again."

Harvey nodded to the girls, but kept his scowl on Asher. "You bring them here to gloat?"

"What did you want me to do? Park them in the alley?"

"Take 'em to Lilith."

"They don't go to her. They're staying here."

Gordon gave Asher a flat look. "At the dance hall."

He nodded.

Gordon's gaze jumped to Emilia and back again. "What for?"

"Entertainment. What else?"

The match in Harvey's hand popped and flared to life as he struck it. He nursed the sputtering flame to the end of a new cigarette dangling from his mouth. "You try to run Lilith out of business, she'll have your throat."

"Not the same kind of business. This is strictly hands-off."

Smoke billowed from Harvey's mouth like a dragon who just found his dinner. He circled Meg and his gaze raked up and down with a full body assessment. "No safeguards. No security. What's to keep someone from running off with one of your girls?"

"You are." Asher tossed Harvey his amulet, then did the same to Gordon. "You're each bound to one of these girls. Since you're here every night, make yourselves useful. You'll be protecting them."

"Whoa, whoa, hang on!" Gordon said.

His voice drowned out by Harvey's booming laughter. "Oh, I'll protect her, but who's going to protect her from me?"

"There's not enough to go around," Charlie groused.

"Sorry, boys. Had to put an extra guard on Liz here. She's an animal." He looked back to the girl wearing a petrified look of surprise as she bobbed up and down in midair. Asher lowered her to the floor with a sweep of his hand, but the look of utter shock remained painted on her face. He slapped her on the back. "Give her a moment. She's gonna warm right up."

"No, they're right. One's missing." Harvey arched a ruddy brow. "Don't tell me one escaped."

Asher looked away with a cold snarl.

"I know you," Harvey persisted. "See something pretty, you take it. So how'd she get away?"

"Doesn't matter. I'm going back for her."

"Uh-huh."

Gordon reached for Emilia's waist and lowered her to the floor with all the poise of a ballroom dance. Sickening, really. The chemistry between those two meshed like childhood friends under the apple tree. He lifted Emilia's wrist and turned it over, then studied the other one. His brow furrowed. "Where's your brand?"

Without a sound, she turned and piled her honey-streaked hair atop her head to reveal the angry burn at the nape of her neck. A geometric, princess design that mirrored the exact pattern of Gordon's amulet.

Gordon moved to trace his fingers along the wound's border, just as Emilia stepped out of reach. He clenched his hand and dropped it to his side, as if suddenly aware of his audience. He turned to Asher. "What do you need?"

"Just the room. They'll rest for tonight."

Asher looked again to the twins, but they were too busy turning Liz this way and that like a pair of curious chimps. Clyde pulled at the neckline of her shirt and peeked inside.

"Hey!" Liz slapped her hands over her chest.

Both men flinched in unison when she thrust out her arm, as if anticipating their due punishment.

Liz gave an exasperated sigh and rotated to show the strawberry-red brand on her inner arm.

Clyde stretched his amulet out for comparison and both men traded a puzzled look.

Harvey's lips curled to a smug grin. "All right, let's see it."

Harvey wasn't a small man by any standard. He had a good eight inches on Meg. But in her levitated state, she did a damn fine job of looking down her nose at him. "I'm not showing you nothin'."

"You want me to find it for you?" Harvey reached for her waist, but jumped back again when she tried to introduce her foot to his manly pride.

67

A flare of determination lit in his eyes. He grabbed her leg before she could make a full retreat, and tugged her to the floor. She hopped once, and staggered forward before crashing into his arms.

"Jerk! Get away." She punched him in the chest.

"Okay, okay," he laughed.

She stepped back looking from one man to another as if ready to take on the next contender.

Asher pressed a fist under his nose to hide his smile. He cleared his throat and cut a meaningful glance to her waist.

Harvey approached her angry puss expression with his palms out. "Look you little bearcat, you've made your point, but you're gonna have to show it sooner or later. Let's get it over with."

He folded up her tight cotton shirt to expose a sun-bronzed midsection...but no brand. His grin widened when he hooked a thumb into her jeans and shot another look to Asher.

Asher looked away. *Go ahead, have your fun...I hope she bites you.*

When the button popped free, Harvey closed the distance between them and looked down.

"The hell!" He tugged either side of her jeans apart and the zipper ripped down. Harvey peered closer to the brand, but even from Asher's vantage point, he could tell the brand didn't fit.

Harvey's attention snapped to Asher. "You did that on purpose."

Meg gave him a sweet as sugar grin as she fastened her pants and side stepped to the twins, exchanging places with Liz.

Asher couldn't contain the snort of laughter.

"Completely by accident."

Harvey's features darkened with festering rage. "You think you're dead now, just wait till I get through with you."

Chapter Six

Conjuring the Prince of Purgatory requires a gathering of impressionable followers, a full moon, and a sacrificial virgin complete with ceremonial costume.

Baila snapped the book shut. She had all that, wrapped in a neat little package called prom.

She stuffed the book into her bag and panned the crowd from her vantage point on the balcony. The impressionable youth was the easy part. When the senior class had learned about Saltair and rumors of Gadspy's ghost, they took the roaring twenties theme to epic heights.

The ballroom glittered with dresses of every color, dripped with fringe and swanky pearls. Stray feather threads of pink and violet caught the evening breeze and danced high above the crowd, swooping and spinning through the air like love-struck confetti. Not unlike the sick flurry that danced around in Baila's stomach.

She smoothed a shaky hand down her thigh-length, cream and gold dress. Nervous? Puh. Baila never got nervous. She couldn't be more prepared. After a wheelbarrow's load of books, notes, and every website imaginable, Baila had the perfect recipe to serve herself on a proverbial platter. All Asher had to do was show up.

Baila moved to start another lap of the perimeter, but the flabby hairball that puddled at her feet tripped her up. She staggered forward with her arms out, ready to crash land on the polished wood floor, when a beanpole of a boy snagged her arm.

"Whoa, are you okay?" He clothes lined her forward momentum, and hung on until she managed to get her feet back under her.

"Fine." She shrugged away and turned to glare at the pint-sized culprit. "Tripped over a dust bunny."

The boy's eyes narrowed. "Sure you haven't had too much to drink?"

Baila gave the boy a flat look. "Oh, you caught me. Punch bowl's been spiked, and I was its first victim."

His expression brightened. "Seriously?"

She angled her head to the buffet table. "Give it a try if you don't believe me."

The boy scurried off without another word, and Baila looked to where Toffee sat nibbling at the ankle strap of her black velvet heels. She shook her foot and dealt him a fierce whisper. "That's a bad bunny."

Toffee twitched his nose, all innocent, as Baila passed. But the moment her back heel was out of reach, the telltale *ka-thump, ka-thump* of his bounding gait followed her every step. She fought the urge to quicken her pace just to put some distance between them.

The sound had been a constant from the moment the bunny had appeared. In the kitchen, the bathroom, even when she left the house—she couldn't get rid of him. How he managed the high-speed chase to prom, she'd never know. He just showed up. Everywhere.

Pity no one else could hear him, otherwise she'd feel justified clomping laps around the floor like a horror-flick bimbo with no sense of direction.

She took a deep breath. For now, she could only tune him out. There were bigger problems hiding here, somewhere.

She stuck close to quiet corners with her ears primed and a hand clutched to the dark amulet around her neck.

A blinding flash from the photographer's nook lit the room. Baila attention caught a flicker of movement from the alcove ahead. The amulet warmed against her skin, and sped her heart to a gallop.

Someone was here.

A second pop and flash of the camera pushed at the shadows again, but they flooded back before Baila could form a clear picture. She eased closer with hesitant steps. Asher wasn't the wallflower type, but he might be trying to lure her from the crowd. If he wanted to settle this privately, fine, but walking into the dark corner made her nerves ticky as a windup toy.

A group of prom goers sauntered into her path. The girls, with rigid, Barbie-doll limbs and flawless, unmoving heads. Baila shot an exasperated glance to the domed ceiling when the group slowed to a grazing rhino's pace.

One girl widened her sapphire-painted eyes. "Can you believe all this?"

Her date bobbed his shaggy head in time with the thumping base. "I know, huh?"

He pointed to the massive window, where a dark archway sat suspended in the lavender sky. "Check it, you can actually see the gateway from here."

"Never been this close before. Hey, you still going to the fence line tonight?" another boy asked.

"Yeah, wouldn't miss it. You?" Shaggy asked.

"I am *so* not going out there," the girl announced.

Shaggy hooked his arms around her and pulled her close to his waist. The Tiffany blue feather plumes in her hair swooped back like a tiny Muppet taking flight. The look on the girl's face said she wouldn't mind following it.

"Don't worry. I'll keep you safe." He stretched his puckered lips toward her.

Perfect. Not only did Baila manage to send her friends off the lemming cliff, but now, the entire senior class might follow. The police department had offered extra manpower at the gate, but even they wouldn't chase after a loony teenager if he wandered too close. They'd lost enough of their work force in the past. Better to go home to their families than to march into a demonic landmine.

She had to get to Asher before anyone else did.

"Excuse me." She stormed through the group with her gaze focused on the dark alcove. Was that an elbow or a shoulder maybe? Too difficult to tell with the black clothing, but something was in there.

She pushed herself onward until she slapped a hand on a narrow, jacketed shoulder.

A freckle-faced boy spun around. His date clutched the front of her dress and shrank deeper into the shadows.

The boy's gloss-smeared lips pulled to a goofy smile. "Oh, sorry. Didn't think anyone would see us here."

"You thought wrong. Now, go on."

When the couple trotted off, Baila looked in horror at the sweep-away gesture she'd been making with her hands. She didn't shoo people. Her mother shooed people. Her *grandma* shooed people. She might be dying, but she shouldn't be aging this fast. How did her life go from young and free, to bitter old make-out Nazi so quickly? She should be the one in that corner, damn it.

"So what's wrong with you? Boyfriend stand you up?"

The muscles between Bail's shoulder blades plucked with irritation, and she narrowed her eyes at the lady standing next to her. Baila forced a grin and raised her voice over the music. "Not exactly."

"Then where is he? It's not right to leave a pretty girl unattended. The men these days..." She shook her mass of dark curls. "Think if they give a girl a pretty bauble, she'll follow him like a lost pup." She scooped the necklace away from Baila's neck and lowered her voice. "Is that what you are, my dear? A pup?"

With all the music, laughter, and clattering heels around them, the accusation should have been scarcely detectable. Instead, it rang through her mind like a bell tower on Sunday morning. With a stroke of shock, Baila moved to lift the amulet away, but the lady closed her scarlet lacquered fingers in a tight grip.

"Never should've told you where to find him. I knew you were up to no good."

"Mildred?" she frowned. "But you're not transparent. Or even a little hazy around the edges."

Mildred gave the amulet a warning tug. "So?"

Baila fisted the cord around her neck and with a swift jerk, the amulet popped free. "I didn't expect to see you this clear." She frowned. "And I didn't call you…"

"People don't *call* me. I don't answer to piddley beckoning. Invite me in or don't, I go where I want." Mildred flung a hand to the packed dance floor below, and her red and purple silk scarf coat billowed around her in a sharp gust of air. "What? You think that hunky boyfriend of yours is the only one strong enough to walk with the living?"

Baila stole a glance to her surroundings and stepped closer to Mildred. Showing up to prom alone was one thing, even for a chaperone, but choosing to consult an invisible friend in front of the entire senior class? There were padded rooms for people like that.

"Speaking of boyfriends—and not that he is. But have you seen him tonight?"

She laughed. "Oh honey, I'm not falling for that twice." She dug into her slouchy shoulder bag. "Now, if you're interested in finding him on your own, I might have something for you." She pressed the withered paper to her double-D chest and worked the tight roll down her body with a rapid flip of her wrist. Baila peered through the blur of water stains to the chicken-scratch map.

The woman's chest puffed up beneath the paper. "Drew it myself."

"Really."

Mildred pushed out a deep sigh. "Hate to part with it. Being an original and all. But you're a nice girl. You'll take good care of it." The rapid-fire blink of Mildred's false lashes followed Baila from head to toe. "It'll only cost you...that tarnished ole necklace."

"Gee, what a surprise."

"What can I say? I'm a sucker for accessories."

Baila angled her head toward the gateway. "I think

I already know how to get there."

"This is a short cut."

She opened her mouth then closed it again. Running short of patience and enough excuses to shoot her down, Baila scrutinized the paper. "But that's a drawing of *Saltair*. Thought you said he doesn't come around here."

Mildred lifted her brows. "Oh, I did, dear. This isn't the Saltair you're standing in. This here is *our* Saltair. The one on the other side."

"You mean the ruins?"

Mildred grimaced. "Yeee, sort of. Your world doesn't really do it justice. Looks nothing like that from our side." She let go of the bottom edge and the paper sprung back to its coiled position. "It's easy to get lost once you cross the gateway, and they prey on the living down there. You'd be foolish to go without a guide."

"What do you mean prey? You mean they actually eat people?"

"Not exactly eat, but they consume them nonetheless—" Her mouth clamped shut to a polite smile, and she lifted her attention to the figure standing behind Baila.

Before she could turn, a warm hand closed around her arm, and her heart shot to her throat.

Baila's mother leaned close and yelled over the thumping base. "Don't tell me those ghost stories going around have you antsy too."

"Course not. You just caught me off guard."

Her mother's face fell serious. "Listen. I want to apologize for dragging you out here."

"It's really no big deal—"

She held up her hand. "No, this was all my doing,

and I take complete responsibility. I don't know what I was thinking. Dragging you out here in your condition. Seeing all these couples together. This can't be easy on you."

Her mom stepped in front of the put-out looking Mildred and pulled Baila into a long hug. Baila offered Mildred a what-can-I-do lift of her hand.

The longer the reassuring pat on her back continued, the more certain Baila became. Her mother hadn't used the touchy-feely ploy in a while. Must be a special occasion. She panned the room of moving bodies and flecks of disco lights until sure enough, she caught two of her mother's coworkers watching them with pitying frowns.

"Mother." Baila's jaw tightened. "I need some air."

"Take all the time you need." Her mother pulled back and cupped a hand to Baila's cheek. "I'll be right here when you get back."

"Great."

Baila hefted her oversized bag to her shoulder and marched from the building with anger frothing in her veins.

"I can't say I blame you," Mildred's voice trailed after her.

"For what?"

"Killing yourself. If I had a mother like that, I'd run myself through with a number two pencil."

"I'm not trying to kill myself."

"Yes, you are. No one walks into purgatory without a death wish. The sooner you admit it, the better off you'll be. You're handing over your life the minute you walk through those doors."

Baila's driving pace wavered a bit but she didn't

stop. For years she'd fought for more chances, more laughter, and more time. Could she really give all that up? Just bury it in the dirt?

For her friends she would. They weren't meant to die like her. They were destined for grandchildren, and rocking chairs. She couldn't let Asher take that from them.

And if he already had? Well, somehow she'd make him give it back.

"This is my stop," Mildred announced.

Baila looked to the three police vehicles standing guard at the fence. "Why? What are you afraid of?"

Mildred lifted her chin. "Nothing. It's just not my place."

"Think if you cross over you'll never come back? Is that it?"

"There's nothing for me over there. Why risk it?" Mildred's face grew somber. "I'm just as alone here as I am there. May as well stick with the familiar. Besides someone's gotta keep this place in order."

Baila nodded to herself. To each their own. Personally, she'd had about all the familiar she could stand.

She stilled the tension in her stomach and meandered closer to the string of police vehicles. Three in total, but they weren't all occupied. The middle car sat vacant, its owner lounging against another patrol car parked further north. With two vehicles distracted, the only threat looked to be the one closest to the fence, and he didn't look happy."

His meaty elbow hung out the open window and the scowl that framed his mirrored shades seemed etched beyond his years.

The distance between the vehicles and the gate seemed workable. One shot. That's all Baila needed. If she could get him to turn his back, she could beat him to the gate.

"Fence line's off limits, Ma'am. You need to step back," he called.

The two officers to the north fell silent. Their eyes turned to Baila. She flashed her biggest smile and turned back to the man in the car. "Ugh, don't call me that. I'm not old enough to be a 'ma'am.'"

The officer whipped off his sunglasses, and his scowl vanished. "Baila Grey. Is that you?" He shoved open the door and stepped out.

Was it? Baila fought the urge to look behind her. She wasn't the girl he knew back in school, but maybe, just maybe she still had a little of that alluring ol' Baila still left deep in her pocket.

She slipped into a sexy tone. "Marty Hunter. Should have known that was you. I thought you got a football scholarship."

Marty's gaze fell to his boots. "You kidding? I could play, but not that well. And my grades were crap."

Something about the warm color growing in his cheeks made Baila want to puff up her chest Mildred style. That was, until he stole a yo-yo glance from said chest to thighs and back again. "Did...you go on a diet or something."

So much for sex appeal. She lowered her head. "Or something."

"You look...good. What you doing out here?"

Not impressing you, that's for sure. She pushed out a sigh and looked back to the building. "Chaperoning."

"Bet that's fun."

"Yeah, I was hoping I'd find someone out here to hang with."

His brows lifted.

"Don't look so pleased."

"Sorry. It's just..." He shot a glance to the other officers. They hadn't moved—thank God, but the one outside the vehicle straightened and crossed his arms over his chest.

"You're not supposed to be here," Marty said.

Baila kicked a tiny pebble with the toe of her shoe. "You mentioned that, but I'm stuck here for the next few hours, just like you." She stole a pleading glance through her lashes. "Cut me some slack?"

Marty stared at her a minute, then his shoulders dropped in defeat. "All right, come on. Let's introduce you to the other guys."

Baila fell in step behind him until they cleared the back bumper of his car, then she cut between his vehicle and the next, and raced for the gap in the fence.

"Hey, hey, hey! Stop right there." The sound of heavy soled shoes pounded the salty turf behind her. The mild slope preceding the fence helped her pick up speed, and with a quick twist of her torso, she squeezed through the gap.

Marty shoved his arm through and swiped at her. His fingernails snagged the side of her silk dress, but she jumped back before he could get a firm grip.

"Don't make me come after you," he warned.

When the two other officers raced down the slope, Marty seemed to remember himself. His hand moved for the taser at his waist.

Baila staggered back. "Do us both a favor. Don't be

a hero. Just let me go."

"You're making a huge mistake, breaking a rule that's made to protect you," another officer said.

Baila turned for the edge of the lake, and ran. The sand grew thick and every step sucked on the heels of her shoes. She peered to where the decrepit building had lifted from the water, but only the mirrored reflection of sunset greeted her.

A small collection of onlookers was growing by the minute outside the prom. Friends were waving each other over to watch the crazy lady off herself.

"Let's talk about this. You don't want to go out there," Marty said.

"Baila Grey, What the *hell* do you think you're doing?" her mother shrieked.

She ignored the sharp cringe that raced down her spine and slipped off one shoe. She tossed it over her shoulder without looking. It hit the bank with a soft thud.

"Honey? Baila." Her mother's voice grew louder, and it jarred with each hasty step.

"Go back, Mom." She removed the second shoe, and started marching forward again before it hit the ground.

"You don't need to do this. You've still got time. You've—"

"Got my whole life ahead of me?" Baila fired back.

The chain link echoed a soft rattle when her mother met the fence, but Baila knew she wouldn't breech it.

"You go in there. Save my daughter right now, you hear me?"

Baila shook her head. Now that's the mother she knew. Never willing to do anything for herself, always relying on someone else's sacrifice. If she didn't succeed crossing over to purgatory, they'd put her in a mental institution for trying. If she did succeed, she couldn't allow anyone else to get dragged down with her.

Baila broke into a full sprint for the gateway, but her pace slowed down to a high-knee lunge as the water crept up her legs. The fence shrieked behind her, and her attention flashed to Marty, who had pushed his way through the gate.

His handsome features twisted with desperation. "Stop!" he yelled.

"Don't follow me, please, it's okay to let me go," she begged as she lunged into the murky water. She clutched her shoulder bag above the water's reach and pumped her legs faster. The tacky lake bottom disappeared. Baila worked toward the gateway with a one armed stroke and the frantic kick of her legs. The rapid slap of footsteps on the shore grew to a deafening thrash as Marty chased her into deeper water.

Gravity seemed to shift there, tugging her closer to the portal and adding strength to distance between her and Marty. The pulling point. The boundary between this world and the next.

Come on. Come on. Her attention locked on the gateway, but the doors were sealed tight. She'd always heard those that stood too close got sucked in. Where's the doorbell? The secret password? Shit, anything!

She looked back to Marty, who's powerful strokes were eating up the distance between them. There had to be a way in. She fisted the amulet until the metal edges cut into her hand. *Work, damn you.*

Her friends were sucked away without an amulet

but they all had one thing in common, the cord. The minute the amulet fell out of Asher's hands, he got sucked away too. She had both pieces of the puzzle, but maybe the answer could be found if she separated them.

Baila wrapped the cord around her fist and tried to tug the amulet free like Asher had done. The frantic pedaling of her legs seemed more than enough to keep her afloat in the salty water, but with both hands occupied, her shoulder bag went under and its weight seemed to pull her down with it.

When Marty's hand clamped over her forearm and jerked her back, the amulet popped free.

Baila wrenched her shoulder and tried to squirm out of his grip.

"Don't fight. We're going back." Marty shoved her head under the water and pulled her back up just as quickly.

The burn of salt water filled her sinuses and she squeezed her eyes shut.

"Snap out of it, or you're going under again."

The sound of grating stone rumbled through the sky and Marty's words rushed together in panic. "We're getting out of here. Move." Marty tugged her backward with each stroke, once, twice.

Too late. The foreign pull of the gateway's magnetism started a brief tug-of-war and slowed Marty's progress. Baila felt a moment of relief as she ripped from his grasp and the world around her shot into a dark abyss of speed and searing wind.

Chapter Seven

The click of Lilith's heels hacked through distant carnival music as she crossed the stone courtyard. The crowd had come out. The over-sized amusement lights buzzed and flickered to life. The air filled with the scent of roasted cinnamon.

And the collectors had returned late. *Again.*

The rollercoaster grew to a deafening roar overhead, then fell away. Its shadow snaked over her with a gust of tepid wind. Her hair swirled up. Her dress fluttered to life and lifted above her knees before falling limp again when the breeze left her. She shot a forced puff of air to the displaced curl on her forehead. It bounced forward again, unhindered, as Lilith rounded the last potted palm tree and snapped an about-face to the steps of the Grand Saltair.

At least this time the boys had brought back a profit. Bagging this many girls in one trip didn't happen often—if ever—and the stir it created would make for a busy night. She needed time to condition, dress, and sedate the girls for harvesting. She could do all that, but it left no time for a much needed trip to the mill.

The extra women would come in handy, but Harvey promised, *promised* the next time he went out he'd find more labor. She had counted on that, and now she'd have to wait for him to take another trip.

Her irritation flared, and she tucked the irksome

curl behind her ear. The pale flesh of her arm caught her attention. She looked again, and then cast a quick glance to her bare shoulder. Great. She scrubbed up and down both arms. Her husband, Alex, the mayor and king of purgatory, adored her coffee-bronze complexion, but her diminishing energy made it dry and ashy around the edges.

When a spirit reached their—uh—prime, it became more difficult to maintain an earth-bound image, and maintenance wasn't cheap. She needed a stronger aura to sap, someone with stamina. Strength.

Purgatory's stingy political circle didn't approve of keeping males at her Doll House. Instead, the women were encouraged to find reliable locals—husbands for support and sustenance. You know, like in the living days. But Alex kept a tight fist when it came to parting with his pilfered energy.

Her stomach soured at the memory of her fledgling months in purgatory. When Alex had leered over her as the room clouded to a thick fog. The cold tang of polish had filtered through her senses when his shoe traced the curve of her jaw. "You're sexy when you're desperate. It pleases me," he had said.

She cast a narrowed glance to the second floor of the town hall building. To the middle window that lit with a rancid, yellow glow. Lilith had been a convert to purgatory. A transplant. Brought here as a human slave, she had earned her amulet by the most despicable of means. But she had no desire to simply fall in line and accept her fate. Alex's time would come. Soon he'd be the one sobbing in the corner, depleted and afraid. But until then, she had to keep her mind and body sharp.

The waifs Lilith peddled at the Doll House might

be adequate for most, but if the staff caught her siphoning her own merchandise, she'd lose her reputation.

She'd managed to convince Alex if he retired, she could set him up a private room at the boarding house. Someplace out of the public eye with all the aura he would ever need. And then some. She knew Alex would be particularly fond of the "then some" part.

If the rumors were true, and the boys managed to bring back an unusual collection of girls, the timing couldn't be better. Now if only she could keep them from screwing it up.

She spied a group of dapper jazz musicians warming for the night's performance. Over the murmuring hoards of dull-faced carnival goers, a saucy drumbeat tugged her interest. Not too unusual for them to be practicing, but the rhythm...She slowed her pace. That song wasn't on tonight's dance card at all.

As she neared the band, thirty pairs of lips seemed to curve in unison. The drummer's heavy rhythm kept time with the sway of her hips. They were teasing her. Lilith toyed with her long strand of pearls and grinned. She exaggerated her sauntering gait. "Why, you naughty boys. Trying to butter me up for a discount?"

"Well, we can hope," called the drummer.

"Where you headed, Ms. Landin?" the base player called.

"To the collectors. Have you seen them?"

The base player cut the heavy downbeat with a quick hand gesture, and the airy carnival tune fell into place again. He turned a puzzled look to Lilith. "Try the dining hall. They're always there round this time."

"Right. Thanks for the tip, Sugar."

"Uh...Ms. Landin?" He angled his head in the opposite direction. "Dining hall's that way."

She laughed and made a quick pivot. Layered ruffles of violet silk fanned the length of her torso. "I knew that. My mind is going in too many directions today."

The base player shook his head. "I don't know how you do it, Madam Mayor."

Yeah? Neither did she and that posed another problem. Not only was her body showing signs of depletion, but her mind as well.

She'd misplaced her master keys twice already this week, and each time, it sent her entire staff into a hand-wringing tizzy. A chunk of metal that large couldn't just disappear. It would've turned up eventually. But ever since Alex declared plans for retirement, her staff had been chicken-littling all over the place. Now the collectors were toying with her too. Not smart, not even cute, and tonight they'd regret it.

When she rounded the corner to the shadowed dining room, her heart skittered. Those good-for-nothing slouches were standing far too close to tonight's prospective headliners.

"Oh, no, you don't. Want time with my girls? You'll pay like everyone else," she said.

Asher stepped into her path and held up a hand.

She shot him a brittle look and shuffled to the right.

He blocked her again. "We need to talk."

"Not now." She looked away but caught him again in the reflection of one of the many floor to ceiling windows that lined the dining hall. His muscular silhouette seemed to contour hers with intimate precision—complete opposites that always seemed to find themselves in an uncomfortable attraction.

Asher had a knack for bad timing. He always tried to soothe her when she became angry, but when approachable, he wouldn't even glance her way. How silly they looked. More like quarreling lovers than stepmother and son.

They were about the same age. Their skin tones and dark hair struck perfect harmony together. If it were him and not his father that had dragged her to this hellhole, things would've been different. Asher had to know that.

He treated her as an equal, not a superior, and he cared for her. Out of respect, he suppressed it of course, but every so often his emotions slipped. A shadow darkened those steely eyes, a show of fruitless hatred for the burden his afterlife had become.

It seemed pure torture for him to visit the Doll House, being so close, yet forced to seek pleasure with another woman. He seemed to openly avoid it. In fact, she couldn't remember the last time she'd seen him there. But Asher never had to worry about his supply of aura. As long as he played the part of collector, he never would. He'd earned that privilege as the mayor's son. But the good mayor wouldn't be around much longer.

Lilith cupped his face. Delicious warmth spread from the faint stubble against her palm. His complexion had taken on a husky glow since the last time she'd seen him. "Got a little some for yourself, did you?"

He frowned and opened his mouth to speak.

"—oh, it's all right." She flashed a quick appraisal to the three women corralled behind him. "The girls don't show it much. After a few hours of rest, no one will know the difference."

"Charlie. Clyde. Take these girls to the house." She waved at the twins before turning to Harvey. "I'd like to say that you've outdone yourselves, but what about the men? More labor? You weren't really expecting to take one of these females to the mill, were you?

Harvey blinked. "Why not? My humans are completely harmless. The males are castrated on site to avoid any detracting behavior. You know what a stickler I am for protocol." He rocked back in his chair and put his hands behind his head.

They both knew he lied, especially about the castration bit. But to dispute it meant putting her supply for high-potency aura in danger. Lilith clenched her jaw at the traitorous heat that flooded her cheeks. "Be that as it may, it's still a rule. Women are strictly for harvesting."

Harvey smirked. "Well, I think Asher aims to change all that. Don't you, old boy?"

"I'll speak for myself. Charlie. Clyde. Don't move the girls just yet."

Lilith's brows shot up her forehead when they actually obeyed him and eased back onto their stools. "You really think these delicate things belong in a silkworm mill?" She angled her head toward the door. "I said. Take. Them to. The Doll House."

"They aren't going to the mill or the house." Asher cut a warning glance to the twins, who looked ready to thump the next person who told them what to do.

"You're joking. Where else could they go?" she asked.

"They're staying here."

No, no, no. Her mind whirled into panic as she

stared at Asher's unyielding expression. "You can't..."

Their economy only revolved around two things, power and more power. The system offered equal opportunity for wealth or poverty, all dependent on one measly little necklace and the amount of aura it could circulate to its owner.

Due to plague of memory loss, Lilith's patrons often "forgot" about their growing tab at the Doll House and were forced to settle debts with their most prized possession. Their amulets.

Or someone else's.

The rich hunted the poor for their coveted necklaces and spent all the profits siphoning more human aura. Over time the energy depleted, and the cycle started over again.

But the more their population shrank, the shorter the cycle.

She had only collected three amulets this week. If her clients shirked their bill for a free night at the dance hall, matters would only get worse. And what if her debtors never came back? Then what?

Her words rushed out in hitching breaths. "You can't. You're not equipped. You don't have the provisions to keep humans here. Besides, they wear my brand and—"

Asher shook his head slow. "They don't wear your brand."

Her mouth hinged open. Poised words caught like a startled mouse in her throat.

Asher's tone remained even. "They're bound to the boys, not you."

Lilith swiped her amulet from Gordon's outstretched hand, which had suddenly appeared over

Asher's shoulder. She dealt Gordon an icy glare. "So you're taking them for yourselves? Is that it?"

Gordon stole a glance to one of the prim little turncoats. He squared his shoulders. "That's right. She's mine now."

Asher gave an exaggerated eye roll. "It wasn't their choice."

Lilith made a slow turn. "Of course not. You were behind all this, weren't you? You and your harebrained schemes. Always out for your own best interest. Taking what you want, when you want it, with no regard for obligation."

She met him nose to nose with a menacing sneer. She didn't want to do it, but she couldn't stop herself. The words seeped hot through her teeth. "Your father won't stand for this, and you know it. There's a price for those who defy our laws, Asher. Not even you can escape that. And you know it better than anyone."

Asher's face hardened to an impenetrable mask.

Lilith knew the sudden change meant she'd hit her mark. She stepped back. "So which one's yours?" The echo of her heels knocked against the walls as Lilith paced a tight circle around the women. "Which one of these little tarts gets tied to the old spindle tree? Which one gets their throat slit tonight?"

Harvey's shoulders bounced with repressed laughter. "Oh, that one? She's not here."

Lilith turned.

"Fraid she got away," Harvey declared.

"Got away? How could she get away?"

She turned. "—Asher, where's your amulet?"

The other men stilled, and a collective shock stretched through the room.

Victory ballooned in Lilith's chest.

This was it, the perfect example for why only she could manage purgatory's throne. And as a bonus, the sweet prince's afterlife would take a dramatic turn. No more fun and wistful games on earth. The naughty boy just got himself grounded.

She canted her head. "Oh, how the mighty have fallen. Tell you what, why don't you stop by the house tonight. We'll get you set up with an account. You can start hunting to cover your tab. In the meantime"—she flung a helpless gesture to the girls—"let me take care of them. These aren't just stray puppies you're dealing with. They require special precautions."

The girl with streaked hair stepped forward. "Excuuuse me? Don't we have a say in this?"

"Quiet, Meg," Harvey called.

Meg's brows drew together with a look of disgust. "Screw you, Harv. You're not the boss of me."

"You see," Lilith continued. "They're already acting up."

"If you expect us to just go along with this crap, you're out of your mind," Meg said.

"I said. Quiet." Harvey slashed out his cord with a flick of his wrist.

She notched her chin up in challenge. "Go ahead. Try it. Tie me again and just see what happens."

Harvey stroked his cord with the pad of his thumb, then looked up through a fringe of chocolate lashes. "You ask for it often enough I'm beginning to think you like it."

"Oh, get over yourselves," Lilith moaned. But the boys seemed to pay no attention.

The twins took position on either side of Meg.

"Beat it." Charlie said.

"She's not your problem, remember?" Clyde challenged.

"How could I forget?" Harvey clamped the cigarette between his teeth and grinned. "But unfortunately, she's making it my problem."

Clyde braced himself in front of Meg. "Your problem is about to get a whole lot bigger—"

"—or smaller," Charlie quipped. With a metallic snap, a small blade flashed in his hand. "—considering I'm about to cut your dick off and shove it down your throat."

Lilith didn't bother to hide the annoyance in her voice. She shouted over the male voices edging to dominate. "There's a lady in the room. You don't talk like that!"

"I'm rather enjoying it," Meg said.

"Puh, you would," Lilith countered.

"That's it!" Asher shouted. "Twins, get those girls upstairs. *Now.* Gordon, I want a word with you. And, Harvey? Please escort Ms. Landin to the mill. I'm sure the two of you have plenty of inspections to work through."

"You're not brushing me off," Lilith said.

Harvey's callused hand touched the back of her arm, but she jerked away. "You give me those girls and you do it now. I don't have time for this. I have a business to run, and you are not going to push me out of it—"

A tell-tale rumble sounded from overhead and drowned out her voice. She paused.

The gateway.

But how?

"Calm down, darling. No one's pushing you out of anything."

Lilith froze at the insidious calm in her husband, Alex's voice. The sight of his lanky silhouette poised in the ballroom doorway, his jet-black fedora tipped to one side. "Now what's the meaning of all this?"

The surprise that seized her tongue still wouldn't let go, and Lilith tripped over her words like they were made from pulled taffy. She turned to Alex, then back to Asher. "He—they're trying to undersell my merchandise. They've got three—"

"Four." Alex nodded.

Lilith tucked her chin. "Four? There's only three." She glanced to the scene behind her, but the twins had already vanished with the girls.

"There must be another. I know I heard the sound. So, who crossed the portal just now?" Alex asked.

Gordon and Harvey exchanged an unreadable look with Asher, and marched for the door.

Alex gave them a passing glance before his gaze turned to his son. "All the collectors are accounted for…?"

Asher stared straight ahead. "Yes."

"So…Who just came through the portal?" Alex asked.

Lilith folded her arms and arched her brow with intrigue. "Well, let's go find out, shall we?"

Asher pinned her with a dark glare, but it failed to counter the greedy excitement stirring in her chest. Oh, this just keeps getting better and better.

****

Asher's determined steps carried him well ahead of Lilith's high-elbowed strut. His father hung back, watchful and unspoken as always, like a rat sniffing out scraps. Just the thought of his father tailing him made Asher's spine itch. He couldn't recall much of the blue-collar father from childhood. Not that it mattered. That man was dead, and the afterlife had a way of stripping a man to his basic elements. Alex Landin whittled down to ego, greed, and not an ounce left to spare.

Gordon and Harvey stood waiting at the embankment ahead of the portal. Toothy grins of delight lit their faces. The tart rasp of Baila's voice grew more desperate the closer Asher came, and their grins only widened.

Asher dealt them a you're-about-to-lose-your-teeth grin of his own. Saltair may have lost its life, but it never lost its competitive edge, and as Coney Island's whored out older sister, its inhabitants thrived on playing dirty. The boys knew that, and the threat of Asher's retaliation wavered on their faces.

"I want to see Asher," Baila demanded.

Asher trudged up the hill of shifting sand. "You sure? Because it's not going to be pretty."

When he topped the embankment, he found a fair-skinned warrior staking claim on the packed earth below.

Was she...? He blinked. No, not naked, but damn close. Her image refined to show a tight, champagne-colored dress, one that blended just enough to be dangerous.

And those legs again. His gaze traced along the scalloped hem that met her upper thighs. He let out a soft whistle.

She must not have heard him, or felt the weight of his slack-jawed stare. She seemed too distracted with fending off her gawky assailant.

Elliott stepped a wide arc around her. His attention shifted first to the spiked heel she poised above her head, then to the necklace in her fist, and back again. "Don't—now, don't do that. You put that thing on and you'll mar that pretty white skin." He made a slow coaxing motion to the chained amulet dangling from her fist. "Give it here, and we'll see if we can't straighten this whole thing out."

Baila edged back. "I don't think so."

Asher could detect the amulet's angry glow even from a hundred yards out. Bright embers of green and yellow floated through the dark stone like fireflies on the wind. And when that thing met skin, it aimed to strike.

"Come on, you don't really want that tarnished ole thing," Elliott said.

Baila's eyes narrowed to tiny slits, and she opened the amulet's chain with her free hand, ready to slip it onto her head.

Elliott gave her an offhanded chuckle, but in a blink, he lunged for the amulet.

Baila jumped back and let go a yelp of surprise. It seemed almost an afterthought when she swung at Elliott with the spiky shoe. The moment it connected with his shoulder, Elliott knocked it from her hand.

She twisted away as Elliott swiped for the amulet.

Asher's gut clenched, and he bounded down the embankment, with heels grinding the moist sand. The uneven ground rose and fell, but Asher kept his eyes zeroed on Baila. The world grew sluggish—his progress included, as he fought to reach her in time.

Elliott's face flooded beet red, and he swiped for

her again.

Baila ducked, and with a shriek of outrage, she shoved at Elliott's torso linebacker style with enough force to knock both of them to the ground. The sound of tearing fabric split the air.

Baila popped back up, ready for another go, but Elliott didn't recover quite as fast. He seemed to forget about Baila. He slapped at his lapels with a muttered curse and looked from one arm to the other. "Now you rip my suit? You people are diabolical."

Baila's attention rounded to Gordon and Harvey on the ridge, then she found Asher. Her eyes grew wide, and soft lips fell open.

Well, hello to you too. He slowed to a trot.

Relief washed over her features, but it didn't last. A frown plumped her lower lip, and her delicate brows drew together. Sure, she meant business, but he couldn't bite back his grin if he tried. That look had all the ferocity of a naked Chihuahua. No wonder that weenie, Elliott, thought he could take her.

"I want a word with you," she said.

"Doesn't everyone today?"

She straightened. A moment of uncertainty shifted in her stance. "I'm here for my friends."

He propped a fist under his chin in thought. "Friends...friends." He dropped his hands to his side. "Sorry, doesn't ring a bell. Bad memory, you know."

"Don't play stupid. Two weeks ago—"

"—Two weeks? Has it really been that long?"

She snapped her mouth shut with a frown.

Ah, now he'd gone and pissed her off again. Man, but he was getting good at this. Time didn't have the same effect here as in her world. It could have been a day or a month ago and he wouldn't have known the difference. The pace of daily life crawled along here in an ageless sky—it practically stood still.

"Remember the Saltair?" Baila demanded. "The wish?"

"The kiss?" Asher wiggled his brows.

"So, the memory returns." The blush on her cheeks deepened and she looked away.

"And it looks like you had that moment replaying like a broken record," he murmured.

Asher's attention flicked to the ridge, where their audience of two had grown to Alex, Lilith, and a chance assortment of the local population.

He turned to Elliott and lifted his voice. "So, what's all this? You going soft on our member's only policy?"

Elliott turned from inspecting his backside and thrust a hand at Baila, who was busy tucking the amulet down her dress.

Asher probably should have stopped her. A gentleman does that kind of thing, but he figured he'd let this one play out. The little bandit deserved some kind of punishment, and since their community frowned on public spankings, he'd let the amulet do his dirty work. For now.

"This little harpy just broke through the portal by herself," Elliott insisted.

"That so?" Asher rounded his attention to Baila.

Her shoulders jumped and a flash of pain scrunched her pretty face. Baila fisted the amulet through the dress and tried to jerk it from her skin. Didn't look like she succeeded. Not only was the dress fit snug to her breasts, but the amulet had a way of bonding to the surface until the job got done. Asher could almost hear the pop and sizzle against her skin as his amulet worked its magic, branding her skin to match the amulet's imprint. If she weren't getting exactly what she'd asked for right now, he'd almost feel sorry for her.

"Ow, ow. Oh, shhhit." Her hopping from one foot to the other grew frantic and she jammed a hand down the front of her dress. She flinched, shook her hand. "Get it off!" She tugged until the chain popped free.

It sailed through the air and landed at Asher's feet, but the amulet wasn't connected. With a final squeal of panic, Baila tugged at the stone through her dress once more, and the amulet tumbled out the bottom.

"What a ride," Asher remarked as he followed the path the stone had just taken. Baila didn't respond. She sucked in a hiss of air, and pinched the cloth away to inspect her seared flesh.

He nodded to her chest. "You all right?"

She lifted her chin and readjusted her stance, even as tears glistened on the edge of her lashes.

Oh hell, now he did feel sorry for her.

He kicked up the cooling amulet from the ground and caught it in his fist. Having grown accustomed to its heat over time, it didn't bother him much. But with the look of bewilderment Baila gave him, he might as well use it to breathe fire.

He stepped close to her and lowered his voice. "You have any idea what you've done? How much trouble you've gotten yourself into?"

"You think I care?" She eyed the amulet's repeated up and down motion as he tossed and caught it. Tossed and caught. "What is that thing?"

"My brand."

"What like Campbell's soup? That kind of brand?"

He gave her an odd look.

"Like a cattle brand?" she tried again.

"That's right." He hooked the amulet to its cord and slipped it over his head. "Consider it your temporary green card. You'll belong to me until you get one of your own."

"When do I get my own then?"

"They appear when you die."

"You have got to be kidding me." She flapped the neckline of her dress back and forth to cool her burnt flesh.

He tossed her an offhanded shrug. "You did it to yourself. Elliott here even tried to warn you."

"Yeah, but you didn't listen, did you? Stupid bird," Elliott muttered.

Asher cut him a warning look. "Hey, we don't talk to the ladies that way."

"Lady? She looks no more significant than common whore," Lilith spat.

"Good. She'll fit right in," Harvey replied.

Lilith's voice edged with irritation over the crowd's rumbling laughter. "How'd you get here? How'd you survive the portal?"

"She's got hardly a scratch on her," Asher's father agreed.

Maybe not, but her hair looked savaged. Her knees were scraped too, and dusted with sand—all the markings of a lover's tryst. Pity he wasn't the first man on site. He'd have a lot less explaining to do as to how she got his amulet.

"We know Asher didn't bring you, so how'd you

navigate the portal?" Lilith asked. Again.

Baila's jaw tightened in offense. "Portal Diving for Dummies Second Edition, chapter nine."

He shook his head. A ghost hunter. Should have known.

Why was it, the most lively of people couldn't seek thrills without death as their spectator? Their constant craving for excitement became their demise in this world, because nothing ever changed. Here, the thrill of cheating death had long run dry. No crucifix or prayer would make this place go away.

"I'm making you a trade. Me for my friends," Baila said.

"Did you really think coming here would get you that?" he asked.

Anger flared in her eyes. "You bet your ass it will."

Asher smirked. "Let's bet yours instead. It's prettier."

Lilith's voice cut shrill across the clearing. "So, what's she doing with your amulet, Asher?"

"Collection methods are strictly classified," he snapped.

"Yeah, well, relinquishing your amulet renders you unfit to collect."

He lifted the stone and chain. "Who's relinquishing?"

"It was out of your hands for an undetermined amount of time. If it weren't for this dumb bird—and you really are dumb by the way—bringing it back to you, it'd be lost to the human world. Your carelessness makes you unfit to carry it."

"My son wouldn't dare squander such a critical opportunity. He's not to blame for this," Alex said.

"No one is," Asher said. "This entire evening was orchestrated. To prove a point."

Baila's lips twisted with disgust. "Oh, you are so full of shit—"

Asher gave her a look that seemed to send poised words skittering to the back of her throat.

An anxious shuffle stirred the crowd, but Asher wouldn't allow time for debate.

"Our methods for harvesting aura have become restrictive. Our technique has gone bland. Profits from the Doll House are at an all-time low."

Lilith's face paled, but Asher continued without pause. "We need a transfusion to stimulate our economy. We can continue our decline, or alter our approach. I chose the latter."

Asher circled Baila with slow, easy steps. "In that respect, I'd like to introduce Ms. Baila Grey. For those of you able to detect human aura, you'll find that hers is unusually strong...potent... addicting. She embodies everything that we hunt for, and she's ours for the taking."

His gaze raked over the length of her body and dipped to the gaping tear at the back of her dress. So that was the tearing sound. Not Elliott. She must've split it when she fell. The curtain of scalloped fabric pulled apart to reveal a narrow ribbon of lace that fanned the upper swell of her backside.

He placed a hand on her back to conceal the rip from view. It might renew his gentleman's card in Baila's eyes, but the urge that brought his hand there had nothing to do with proper etiquette.

Life hummed against his palm with the rise and fall of each anxious breath. His fingertips tingled with the urge to slip his hand inside her dress.

Her breathing stilled.

"I know I'm interested," he said to the crowd.

Her back snapped straight, and she dealt him a warning glare from over her shoulder.

He continued his perusal with a silent snort.

The crowd wasn't privy to the same view he had, but they liked it just the same. Some members looked away and cleared their throats, while others—like Gordon and Harvey, stared openly. The mounting lust for aura hung thick in the air. It made him want to shove her behind him and take on the entire crowd like a rabid grizzly.

But he couldn't.

To preserve his own existence and the lives of these girls, he had to sell his "new plan" to the greediest bastard in all of purgatory—his father.

"Let's make one thing clear," Lilith said. "These women will not be kept to satisfy your own urges— which brings to light another issue..." She jammed a finger in Asher's direction. "She's bound to him now." She turned to the crowd and raised her voice. "They're all bound to one of the collectors. Not me."

Asher's eyebrows lifted in innocents. "Who better to protect them?"

"It's grounds for exile!"

Alex settled a hand on Lilith's heaving shoulder. "Darling? Let the boy speak."

When Lilith finally pursed her narrow lips closed, Asher's gaze flew skyward in quick reprieve. "As I was saying, we need to put women like Ms. Baila here in the open to help funnel new clients to the Doll House. Drum up a little more interest."

"My girls solicit at the dance hall every night," Lilith argued, earning herself a squeeze from Alex's hand.

Asher flung her a dismissive glance. "They're locals. Too pushy, and it's getting you nowhere. Let's be honest, they are only looking for one thing."

A collective mummer of agreement rolled through the crowd, but quickly trailed by feminine huffs of outrage. Careful. Don't stir a hormonal upheaval, keep them playing into your hand.

"They want the same thing we all want," he clarified.

"My girls are real, aura-soaked humans. They will work under a strict hand's-off policy that'll pose no threat to a man's amulet. New clients will become more comfortable, and eventually, work to feed their curiosity. And we'll send that healthy curiosity right to the Doll House."

"How will these women cooperate without sedation? Couldn't they just cut and run?" Alex asked.

"The collectors will form a barrier around Saltair. The women won't leave without escort."

"This seems a well-thought-out plan. Good job, my boy," Alex said.

Asher clenched his teeth at his father's familiar nod of pride. He didn't want the crown of purgatory or to fatten that old man's jewelry box, but he couldn't let Lilith take over either. That would spell misery for them all.

The scamper of tiny, clawed feet pulled Asher's attention to the portal's pliable wall. "Bring somebody with you?"

Baila's response came slow and uncertain. "Not

exactly."

Elliott stomped to the portal and shoved one leg inside, then his fist. He angled his body, ready to pull himself through, when he let out a shriek.

He tried to jerk his leg back with quick twitching movements, and his face pinched with pain.

A tawny colored rodent with large dark eyes squeezed through the gap between the portal and Elliott's knee.

The man jerked his leg free and screamed like a little girl, and the animal bounded from the portal after him.

If there were a kitchen stool, Elliott would be dancing on it. "A rat. A monster rat just tried to eat me!"

"He's a rabbit," Baila corrected.

The "rabbit", as if sensing Baila's voice, made a quick pivot and raced into her arms.

Baila hefted the tubby rodent to her chest. "He's not transparent anymore. He's whole." She tipped her cheek to his fur.

"He's in this world now. We play by different rules," Asher said.

"First the girl, now her pet. What's next? Her house?" Lilith asked.

Baila threw her a brilliant grin. "Yeah, heads up. It'll probably land on you."

"Shut it," Asher snapped.

"You really think you can control them." Lilith said. Not a question…a threat.

Asher flashed his most charming smile. "Ab-so-lutely."

Now only one question remained. How long would

it take before Baila tested that theory?

Alex lifted his voice. "All right Asher, you're on. But this trial will be conducted under strict supervision. The women may be siphoned only as punishment, and to keep them docile."

A loophole. Surprise, surprise. And guess who planned to assign himself as punisher, no doubt.

His father turned. "Lilith, I trust you've kept you staff healthy enough to manage a surge in business?"

Lilith straightened. "Of course."

He gave a noncommittal lift of his shoulder. "Asher, keep your amulet until we see the end result. If we run short of girls at the Doll House, you'll make another run. I take it, with the abundance we've seen today, there should be plenty of bodies to bring over."

Asher nodded. It seemed a growing trend. With this many girls missing in such a short time, there were bound to be an outpouring of mourners and candlelight vigils—all ripe for collecting.

Alex addressed the crowd with pointed glances. "I have until the inaugural session three weeks from now to name a successor. If Asher's prospect turns beneficial, he will become purveyor over purgatory. If he fails, the women will be handled, the men exiled, and Lilith will take the title." He turned to Lilith. "Are you both satisfied with the terms?"

Lilith set her shoulders and gave a swift nod.

Asher lifted an insolent brow and followed the same gesture. Let the games begin.

Chapter Eight

Baila topped the stairs to a sweltering gold and fuchsia hotel suite with diamond wallpaper and three twin beds dripping with blinding-pink, silk sheets.

One red light short of a roaring whorehouse, but then everything looked that way here, even the exterior.

When she first approached the building, the contrast between this Saltair and the one in her world became obvious.

Onion-shaped domes capped the fortress of turrets at each corner of the building—those looked familiar. Except for the magenta checkerboard pattern that had been painted on. If you could call that painting. The layers looked glopped on like melting ice cream.

The hundreds of key-shaped windows were still there. Even the massive oblong structure formed at the center seemed vaguely familiar. Bright mango, but otherwise familiar. Aside from the color, the original Saltair, in all its morbid glory, looked twice the size of the current replica. And it felt twisted and overdressed, like a formidable Taj Mahal from hell. She couldn't find a pastel in this rainbow migraine if she tried.

Baila stopped short when she entered the top-floor suite and her gaze landed on Meg, Emilia, and Liz. They huddled together near the lone, narrow window with their heads bent in silence.

"Hey," she whispered.

Emilia jerked to attention, and her eyes grew wide. "Where've you been?" She fisted her ankle-length dress and rushed across the floor in a flurry of iridescent navy fabric. Meg and Liz followed like a trio of gothic bridesmaids.

Toffee seemed to recognize the circle closing around him, and he sprang free from Baila's arms. He dropped to the floor with a loud thump and scampered under the nearest bed. A sharp clang sounded near the headboard.

Baila closed her eyes. "I swear that bunny's got brain damage by now."

"Of course he does. He followed you here, didn't he?" Emilia pulled her into a lung-squeezing group hug. "We thought you escaped."

"I came back for you guys," Baila rasped.

Emilia held her at arm's length and blinked at the moisture that brimmed in her eyes. She paused and her tone dropped. "What? Why would you do something so stupid?"

"Hey, I couldn't just leave you here."

Emilia pushed out a soft snort and a tear raced down her cheek. "We're pretty much a lost cause."

Baila swallowed the lump forming in her throat. If only she could unravel those words and pretend they'd never been said.

Had they already given up? The three friends that kept her life stitched together?

She shook her head. "How could you think that? You can't let them get to you. If Asher and his goons can leave this place, there's got to be a way out."

"Aaaand any idea how to find that?" Meg asked.

"I'm working on it."

An army of heavy footsteps plodded up the stairs.

Baila ducked to tighten their circle. The words rushed from her mouth in a desperate whisper. "If they don't have enough women for the Doll House, they'll go back for more girls. That could be our best chance for escape."

Liz frowned. "You want them to drag more people down here? That's cold."

Baila looked to the scuffed wooden floor. "Is there another diversion we could create?"

"We could start a fight," Emilia offered.

Meg smacked her fist into her left palm. "Fist fight or cat fight?"

Baila grinned. "Easy, Tiger. If we get caught fighting, they'll probably send us to jail. Or punish us. The whole aura siphoning thing doesn't sound all too comfortable."

"It's not," Liz admitted, rubbing the pale impression on her wrist.

Meg covered the area between her legs with both hands and grimaced. "You think that's bad, you should hear what they do to the men they bring down to work the mill."

Baila opened her mouth to ask for explanation, but Meg jumped in. "You want them to fight each other then?"

"That might work, but how can we do that?"

"—You can stop scheming and finish getting dressed," Harvey replied from the doorway. He backed a fourth bed frame through the door with shuffling steps, while one of the twins brought up the rear— Clyde or Charlie, she wasn't sure which. They both looked the same.

Asher followed, with a saggy, discolored mattress that longed for a dumpster. Gordon and the second twin were close on his heels with a pile of fabric and two heaping bags of groceries each.

"Can't you use your floaty powers for lifting all that?" Bails asked.

"No reckless use of powers within city limits. Only in case of emergency." Gordon swung his bags onto the bed and slipped a small note pad from his vest pocket. "Okay...makeup, perfume, deodorant, tampons, straightening iron, hair spray, Midol, and"—his brows lifted—"bondage rope."

Meg smirked. "Harv's right. I do like being tied."

Harvey lowered the frame in place as if it were the most interesting hunk of rust he'd ever seen.

Gordon offered Meg a not-so-apologetic smile. "Sorry, no rope. You're all on suicide watch till you learn to behave. The necessities are easy to come by. The rest you'll have to do without. How about a candy bar instead?"

"What is it with you and candy bars?" Liz demanded.

Meg winked at the twin holding the bags and goofy grin. "That's okay, we'll improvise."

"Whoa, whoa, whoa. What's all this?" Baila jabbed an accusing finger at the bag. "You haven't actually been making plans to stay here? Where'd all this come from?"

Emila's retort seemed flat and emotionless. "Back home. Gordon here is the Acquisitions Specialist, apparently. Anything you need, he gets."

"Within reason." Gordon clarified.

Emilia looked away. "A one-way ticket outta here

sounded pretty damn reasonable to me."

"What about my iPod?"Liz asked.

"Got that too." Gordon said.

"Is that a necessity?" Harvey drawled.

Liz gave him a smarmy look. "Yes, it's a necessity."

"Are candy bars a necessity?" Meg countered.

Gordon touched the pen to his tongue and poised it on the paper. "They are around here. A hot commodity and pretty effective reward system I'd say...Bails? Anything you need?"

She snapped to attention, and her line of sight flashed from Gordon to Emilia and back again. How did he know her nickname?

"Bails." Emilia ignored her look of confusion and gave a coaxing nod. "You need something else?" Meg and Liz turned to Baila with an apprehensive look, and she knew what they were getting at.

She wouldn't last long without her pain pills. The unexpected headaches she suffered were enough to cripple, but she couldn't let on about her terminal illness. Only moments ago she'd been proclaimed the bright and shiniest of all. She might be stuck here, but the barter was still on. She couldn't let it tarnish. *Not now.* She gave her friends a faint headshake and turned to Gordon. "Just my bag. I lost it when I entered the portal."

"Easy enough." He made a quick scribble and snapped the notebook closed. "All right then. Showtime, ladies."

A sick flurry warmed Baila's stomach. Already? But they just got there. She didn't want to face those washed-out locals again. The hungry look in their eyes made her spine shrivel. The sudden urge to knee Asher in the balls and run like hell must've registered on her face.

His calculating gaze hung in an uneasy silence and his voice fell soft and even. "Boys, take your girls down stairs and show them the routine."

When Baila turned to follow, Asher held up his palm. "Not you. You're not going down like that." When the others shuffled out, he stabbed a finger at the sheet strung up in the far corner of the room. "Strip."

"Uh—no."

He angled his head in challenge, and his jaw line tightened.

Baila motioned for the dark dress in his fist. "I'm a big girl. I can dress myself."

"Suicide watch, remember?" He pushed the door until it snapped closed. "I'm not going anywhere."

"I thought you made the rules."

"It's a good rule. Why would I break it?" With a twist of her shoulders, he spun her around and gave her a shove at the small of her back. "Get your wiggle on, we don't have all day."

She shuffled a few steps and grimaced over her shoulder. "Get your what—?"

A heavy fist pounded outside the door.

"Go," he said.

Charlie's voice shouted from the hall. "Band strikes in twenty."

Asher angled his head toward the door. "We'll be down."

She ducked behind the draped sheet that hung between them. It didn't hide much. The cord that the sheet dangled from only met her collar bone—she glared over the sheet, then to Asher. "Can you see through this?"

His only response came in the form of a quiet snort. A mix between "if only" and "why would I want to do that?"

Either way, Baila had her answer. She shifted the torn prom dress over her hips.

Unjust. Purely unjust. Ripping her dress was one thing. Now he aimed to steal it from her. What did he want with it anyway? It was just a prom dress. A heaven-tailored, hung like liquid gold prom dress.

Her voice turned bitter. "You can wait outside. Being here won't make me go any faster."

Asher's attention lowered to the three-foot gap between the sheet and the floor. He traced her movements as the dress slid down, and she stepped from the pile of cream one foot at a time.

"How do you know about me?" he asked.

"What do you mean, everybody knows you. You're Gadspy's ghost."

He shook his head. "The amulet. How did you know to take it?"

"I guess I just put two and two together. Why?"

Asher didn't respond, but the probing look he gave made her heart want to scamper from her chest and steal Toffee's hiding spot under the bed.

"Isn't there anything else you could be doing?" she demanded.

He angled his head for a better view under the sheet. "Probably."

She kicked the dress to Asher with a huff of irritation.

He pushed himself from the door, and draped a

navy blue shift dress over the clothesline. "I take it the other girls have brought you up to speed?"

Baila refused to answer. She tore the dress from under his hand and the whisper of Dupioni silk rushed over the edge of the chest-high sheet between them. "This is hideous. You know that, right?"

It looked identical to what the other girls wore, but the fabric slid like warm butter through her fingers. Its every movement danced with flashes of purple and green, as if it had an energy all its own.

Hideous? If that wasn't the biggest lie ever told. Sounded convincing, though didn't it?

Asher frowned. "It's standard issue, Baila. You don't get special requests." His attention dipped to her breasts.

"They call me Bails—and stop peeking." She stepped closer to the sheet to thwart his wandering gaze. The static-charged cloth pressed to her curves and clung there.

Asher grinned. "Don't need to."

She gasped and peeled away the cloth. She wanted to jump into the dress and yank the straps over her shoulders fire-drill style, but knowing what waited downstairs, and knowing that Asher was pushing her toward it, gave her every excuse to stall for time. She pulled the pins from the remaining section of hair that hadn't tumbled free, and sifted through her wavy curls.

"You go by your proper name here." Asher said. "No more nicknames, they're not formal enough for your line of work."

When Asher reached for her shoulder, she inched back. He flicked her an impatient look and reached again. "Your outfit isn't suitable either." A whisper soft touch met her shoulder before he pulled back a chubby gray moth for her inspection. "Clothes moths are a plague around here. Your flimsy material would turn to Swiss in one night."

"The attack of your little critter friends might work on other girls, but I have pretty good aim with a shoe."

"I don't control them." His gaze lingered over her bare shoulders where his fingers had just been. "They behave just the same as every stupid creature here. They follow food. And light." He gestured to the stained-glass window behind her, which had become dark and occluded with a mass of fluttering wings. "To them, and everyone else here, you are both."

Baila opened her mouth, but the words disintegrated on her tongue when Asher lifted the fistful of her prom dress to his nose. He closed his eyes, and his chest expanded with a deep, drawn-out breath.

What made *this* guy so magical that he rendered every stupid female speechless? She cleared her throat. *Hard.* "You sure it's the moths I have to worry about?"

He didn't respond. Asher probably meant to rile her by stealing her clothes.

And it worked, damn it.

But the heat that warmed her cheeks couldn't touch the inferno waiting below the surface. She knew that feeling. It wasn't good.

Asher fed her curiosity before, and now that she had a taste, she couldn't get him out of her system. The urge to experience him would nudge her little by little until she finally took the plunge.

She clamped her hands on the clothesline. "Feel free to take that home tonight. Enjoy it while you can, because that's all you're getting."

His lashes swept up with a dark challenge seeped in silver-gray eyes. "Don't let it go to your head. I've got three more of you to choose from. I'm not picky."

"If you so much as even breathe on my friends wrong..."

Asher lifted his brows. "—You'll what? What are *you* going to do to *me*, Baila? Come on, I'd love to hear it."

Baila's stomach flipped, but she refused to lower the stubborn tilt of her chin.

"You're screwed, doll," he cooed. "Even if you leave this place, you're never leaving purgatory." He stepped close and dangled the amulet in front of her nose. "Without one of these, you can't go anywhere."

She swiped for the amulet, but Asher lifted it over his right shoulder and out of reach. He lowered his face within inches of hers and grinned. "Ah-ah."

The smell of frost and sandalwood clung to her senses, but she shoved it away with a forced breath from her nose. Baila stretched against the curtain on the tips of her toes, and the thin material of her bra grated against the clothesline.

Or better yet... Baila pressed herself even closer. The tender flesh of her inner arm grazed his jaw bone and she angled her mouth within dangerous proximity.

Baila fought the excitement writhing up within her and drew in a heavy breath. She released it slow, hoping the warmth would mingle over his lips. Give him a taste of his own medicine. It had worked once.

She sprung for the amulet.

On her second swipe, Asher's free hand hooked around her back and trapped her against him. His mouth swooped down like a hawk after prey and his lips crushed against hers. The cool press of his mouth warmed on contact.

Asher swallowed her yelp of surprise when he angled his head and thrust his tongue in to taste her. A viper's strike of moist heat shot through her system.

He jerked her one-step forward and the clothesline snapped.

The sheet sagged around her and she grabbed for the section caught between them. She tried to twist away, but thick bands of muscle flexed around her, and Asher pinned her arms to his chest.

He stroked a firm hand down her spine. His touch all power and demand, as it slid over the curve of her backside. Sparks chased over her skin and she arched her back in a feeble attempt to escape. His mouth continued to work against hers, diving and retreating in a spellbinding rhythm.

The temptation to follow his pace took over. Sure he scared the hell out of her, but second chances didn't come often, especially for Baila. She had to taste that power again—to take in every bit he offered. It belonged to her, every inch of it. She asked for this—for him. And she deserved it.

His roving fingertips brushed mere inches from the pulsing core between her legs. She fisted his shirt and sucked in a gasp. God, why did everything in this cursed place have to be made of silk?

Baila kept hoping he would pause or at least slow down. It wasn't happening. He forced her leg up, and wedged himself between her thighs.

Too far, too fast. Panic spiked when he rocked against her heated flesh, and forced her legs further apart. Every muscle in her body clenched as the hard ridge of Asher's erection stroked against her.

Then she felt the pull.

The flood of warmth that consumed her, melted the strength from her muscles, and Asher seemed to draw on it somehow. The heat pulled from her body and a bone-aching chill slipped into its place. But the moment her muscles went slack, Asher let go.

She stumbled away on rubbery legs, and her foot tangled in the fallen sheet. Her backside hit the ground with a heavy thud and enough force to rattle her teeth.

Asher's chest rose and fell with ragged breaths and a gleam of triumph sparked in his eyes. "You're not calling any shots here, I am. You may think you've got something over me, but I can handle you just fine. In fact, I'll handle you any time you ask for it."

****

One distinct laugh rose above the others. Deep and warm, it carried easy over the nimble jazz music and a sea of rolling conversation. Baila didn't have to guess who it belonged to. Her fists clenched, knuckles aching.

"So, how about now? Still got a thing for him?" Emilia asked.

She scowled at her sister. "Are you kidding?" She never wanted to punch someone more in her life. Asher had to feel it coming too, because he hadn't made eye contact all night. He lounged in a dim corner, throwing back one drink after another and trading stories with all the other pin-striped bar slugs.

"You're staring..." Emilia said.

"Shut up." She narrowed her vision through spiky lashes. "I'm trying to strangle him by the power of my mind."

Emilia snorted. "Let me know how that goes for

you."

"Look, look, look, here comes another one," Meg said.

A man with a cane, hat, and narrow mustache slapped Asher on the back and gestured to Baila with an easy smile.

She couldn't make out what Asher said to the man before draining the remnants of his glass, but it wasn't encouraging.

The man's smile turned false, then slipped away all together. She'd seen that look over a dozen times tonight.

Asher had turned him down.

Baila rounded to Meg's table behind her. "And what are you so excited about? You want to be handed to one of those pasty-faced sickos?"

Meg propped her chin on both fists. "No...it's their perseverance. It's fascinating. You'd think with those daggers of fury you've been throwing, they'd give up by now. Maybe we should hold up voting cards. You know, give them some rating system to shoot for."

"It's not a hard call. Just look at them," Baila said. The undercurrent of greed seeped through them all. She couldn't see it, but she felt it. The same urge that chased her up dark stairwells as a kid. She could sense which ones were dangerous. And they all were.

Only the collectors looked safe, approachable— probably the reason for getting that job to begin with. Or maybe they'd sated themselves enough to only appear safe.

Baila returned her gaze to Asher's hulking profile. His olive complexion took on a rich bronze after the dressing room incident, and his posture looked massage parlor made—or bedroom made in their case, only they hadn't gotten near the bed.

She cleared her throat and looked away. Yep, he looked pretty damn sated, even from half the room away.

She swiveled the crystal goblet between her thumb and forefinger. She had a decent throwing arm, could probably nail him between the shoulder blades. If only she had a clear shot.

The massive Roman clock overhead struck the three hour mark, for what felt like the millionth time, but the music hadn't stopped once. It flowed seamlessly from one melody to another, and the jittery bounce of fringe and coattails only increased.

The smell of warm bread and ham that had first met Baila had become overpowered by thick perfume and cigarette smoke. Tables were crammed to overflowing—all except the four reserved for Baila and each of her friends.

With Gordon standing guard nearby, every person approaching to converse, or even borrow a chair, got turned away with a critical shake of his head.

"This outpouring must've been more than they anticipated," Baila mused.

"Think so?" Emilia asked.

"Why else would they cram us back here?"

Liz's chair creaked as she shifted to one hip, then the other. "Maybe, they're just waiting to set up the pen. Then they'll grease us up and turn us loose like one of those old pig-chasing contests."

Baila hardened her stare to match the looks from a vibrant parade of young women sauntering past. "Whatever they're planning, I wish they'd get it over with. I'm tired of being gawked at." Her back and forth motion of the glass grew agitated. "Hey, Candy Man?" She tossed the contents of her glass at a nearby palm. "Can I get some more water?"

Gordon turned with his hands clasped politely in front of him.

She peered at the bottom of her glass. "If you'd give me something stronger I wouldn't go through it so fast."

"No kidding," Emilia agreed. "We look like a bunch of speed-dating ugly chicks. No one even wants to spend time getting us drunk."

"Or feed us." Liz's fork clattered onto her plate. "This slop is disgusting. Everything tastes the same. Like varying textures of spam." She smacked her lips. "Got any salt?"

"Oh good idea," Emilia scoffed. "Ghosts have an aversion to salt"—she lifted her brows at Gordon— "Kind-a like slugs."

Gordon unlatched the velvety rope and stepped inside. "You're talking again."

"We're bored. It's what friends do," Emilia replied.

Gordon shielded his heart with both hands. "What are you saying? We're not friends anymore?"

Emilia tipped her head with a sweet-as-sugar grin. "Were we ever?"

"Interesting question." Baila looked from Emilia to Gordon and back again. "Up until now, you two were peaches and cream. What happened?" She paused. "You two met before, haven't you?"

Silence stretched across the room.

"When?" Baila demanded. She turned to Emilia and jabbed a thumb toward Gordon. "Is *he* the reason you stopped conjuring?"

Color crept into Gordon's cheeks, and in that moment Baila understood. She sucked in a gasp. "Oh. My. God. He took advantage of you?"

"More the other way around," Meg snickered. "She—uh—went after his Almond Joy if you know what I mean."

Baila sat back. "What? You can't be serious. You totally went for candy and I missed it? Where was I?"

"Obviously getting a little of your own," Emilia fired back. She propped her elbows on the table and let her chin drop onto her palms. "Doesn't matter. Didn't work anyway."

"Oh, hang on—" Baila started.

Gordon jabbed a finger at Baila. "Quiet. Both of you."

Emilia shot Baila a warning look.

She assessed the unhinged rope in Gordon's hand, then the faint dimple in his cheek and mass of glossy, blonde curls. Between the two of them, she'd listen to her sister, but how could anyone take orders from Drill Sergeant Ken and his atomic halo?

He angled his head in challenge, as if sensing her thoughts. "I'll say it again. This isn't a game. In case you haven't noticed, you've missed your reservation at the Doll House. They're not processing you. For now. No chains. No sedation. But that doesn't mean they won't change their minds. Keep acting unruly and you'll ruin it for everyone."

Baila postured in offense. "*Unruly?!*"

"—Do not talk to anyone—even each other. Do not touch anyone. Don't let anyone touch you."

"Oooh-kay." Baila made an exaggerated eye roll.

"Remain in your collector's sight at all times. If you can see him, he can see you," he continued.

Baila stretched a hand to scrutinize her bitten-to-the-quick nails. Best to pretend she didn't hear that last one. No way in hell—uh, purgatory, did she plan to follow it. She stole a glance to Asher—he didn't care if she were in sight, why should she?

Her chair clattered away from the table. "You know, Gordo, a handful of mannequins would have been easier. They don't have to pee."

"Me too." Meg jumped up from the table behind her.

"We should all go. It'll save you some trouble." Emilia admitted. "Otherwise, you're going to have a pretty big puddle at your feet."

Gordon looked from one girl to the next and then closed his eyes. "Fine. Around the bar, first door on your left. You have five minutes. Then I'm coming after you."

Curious onlookers seized the opportunity of a moving target, and their gazes trailed after the girls, some coupled with excited whispers, while others stayed cold and watchful—a jackal's den of artificial humanity. The primitive drive to sustain wasn't any different from the animals Baila met in East Africa. They could dress it anyway they wanted, but the feral desperation still lay under the surface.

Experience proved that her best option was to back away. The clench of her stomach couldn't agree more. But she'd been backed in that corner all night, and where had it gotten her?

Nowhere.

Baila took a deep breath. New strategy. She'd

make herself as big as possible, and not show an ounce of fear.

She dropped into a down-beat swagger as she crossed the floor with heels clicking and hips swinging like Aphrodite on the prowl. Baila didn't have her sister's gift. Hell, she didn't even share the same body type anymore, but she had a way with giving a mood what it called for. She knew how to set up the picture and let nature take its course.

The girls followed her lead in single file with Gordon scowling at their heels.

Her path neared the front entrance, earning a faint twitch from Harvey's eyebrow. He angled his massive profile to guard any chance for entry or escape and his biceps twitched as he tightened the fold of his arms.

She smirked. Strolling out the front door hadn't been the plan, but with the sudden show of opposition, her ego swelled to twice its size. A human, walking among them without restraint, seemed the highlight of their evening. Oh, but Baila had only begun.

She slipped behind Charlie unnoticed and paid the band a feasting glance. The sway and slash of his conducting motions drove the music, but the gradual pull of the band's attention left his sharp-handed instructions without an audience.

The music wavered out of rhythm.

With a snap of his wrist, Charlie threw his conducting rod end-over-end. The rod impaled in a horn player's chest and wobbled from side to side. The man jerked it free and gaped at the crimson stain growing on his tuxedo shirt.

"Next time it's your eye," Charlie warned.

Baila bit back a laugh, but Meg couldn't seem to

contain hers. When the sharp sound of her delight rang out, Charlie spun the full 180 degrees to face them. He frowned in disbelief.

When the girls skirted the bar, the other twin angled his head with mischief. "Where you girls off to?"

"Ladies' room. Care to join?" Baila asked.

He tucked his chin back, caught somewhere between horror and intrigue. His gaze jerked to the overflowing drink he'd poured. "Uh, thanks for the offer, but I'll pass."

Meg slapped a palm on the bar. "How about three shots on the double then?"

He shook the spilled liquid from his hand and nodded. "That I can do."

"Alcohol dims the aura," Gordon said. "No drinking on the job."

"Can't talk. Can't drink. Exactly what can we do?"

He flicked his glance to the ladies' room. "You can pee, apparently."

Baila turned for the ladies room, but slowed her stride to take in the hushed conversation as Clyde leaned over the bar to Gordon. "They're all going together?"

Gordon offered a careless shrug. "They threatened to puddle me."

"And you believed them?"

"What, you want proof? You know how they are. One goes, they all start going."

The argument turned fuzzy as Baila passed Asher's table, and her thoughts charged with awareness.

Thick bands of shoulder muscle bunched under his shirt, and he turned from the man vying for his attention—a man too bent on pleading his case to notice the commotion around him. Asher's eyes were flat and impassive as he watched her. He leaned back in his chair. Waiting.

She meant to level that same look back at him, but her gaze melted to his lips, the same lips that sent her body burning only hours ago. The heat of that kiss came rushing back, and it formed a tight coil in her belly.

His mouth twitched.

"Baila." Emilia prodded her shoulder.

She snapped back to reality and made a pivot for the girl's room with an I-meant-to-do-that look to her sister. As if Em had any room to talk. The clack of heels echoed off cracked tile the moment they pushed past the swinging door.

"I can't believe you already knew him, Emilia. What kind of game were you playing?!" Baila rounded on her sister.

"Not *now*," Liz insisted.

"Yes, now." Baila scowled at Emilia, whose complexion grew paler by the second. "You set me up."

"You wanted to be set up!" Emilia fired back.

"Well—yeah but not that way. Not with all of this." She shoved an open hand gesture to the door.

Emilia straightened her shoulders. "It's wasn't supposed to be *all this*. It wasn't even supposed to go this far. Gordon and I had a deal. He said he'd come alone and make your acquaintance. That's it! You wanted some excitement, and that's all it was going to be. How was I to know he'd go back on his word?"

"Um… He's a friggin' ghost! What did he have to lose?"

A flash of hurt chased across Emilia's features just before she looked away. "Apparently nothing."

"Sisters go through the same dating pool all the time," Meg reasoned, slinging an arm over each girl. "Em was only trying to help." Meg urged the girls closer, for a make-up hug.

Baila looked away in protest, but she could already feel her resolve crumble. "Please don't tell me, you were all in on this?"

"If only," Meg snorted. "I never would have chosen Gordo to do a man's job."

"It *doesn't matter*," Liz insisted. "We need to focus on getting out of here."

Baila's hope lifted at the sight of a narrow, beveled glass window. "There," she whispered and locked the door behind her.

A hollow grating sound sent her heart racing as she slid an upended garbage can under the narrow opening, and climbed up. She stretched, but her fingertips could only graze the ledge.

"Here, let me." Meg traded places, laced her fingers together, and crouched down. "I'll boost you."

Baila's steps grew shaky climbing up a second time, and she grasped the windowsill with both hands. The hinges had grown thick with coats of paint and rust. She wiped the moisture from her palm and set to working the lever back and forth, back and forth. Shavings powdered the windowsill. The metal cut into her hand.

"Hurry," Meg whispered.

The lever cleared with a metallic squeal and Baila threw open the window. Carnival music swarmed into the room. Fat, colored lights from the Ferris wheel and merry-go-round swirled below with the tepid breeze. Two stories up and a concrete landing. Perfect.

Baila leaned forward to scan the building's facade, but the view rippled in front of her. She reached out. A cold, invisible mesh of some kind pushed back against her hand. The more she pushed, the stronger it resisted. The world beyond the window wavered and bent.

"It's no use. We're netted in somehow."

"Force field," Emilia added.

Baila's lips stretched in a wry grin. "Thanks." She pushed out a heavy sigh. "We've got to find a real door and slip out with some of the locals."

"So, back to plan A then?" Liz asked. "How are we supposed to create a diversion with that many eyes on us?"

Baila spoke over her shoulder as she climbed down. "Make them want to look away. You saw those women. Not everyone wants us here." She dusted off her hands. "If we can build up the opposition, and take away what the others came for, all eyes will turn on the collectors. They'll be too outnumbered to keep focus on us."

She looked to each of her friends. "First objective, we have to dim our aura by any means necessary. We'll get our hands on whatever booze we can find and play up the rest. Emilia, you're the only one of us who can see aura."

Her sister nodded. "I'll tell you when it's enough. It won't take much for the rest of us, but Baila, you're a freaking glow worm."

"I'll improvise."

Baila pushed open the door and her friends scattered.

Meg pulled herself onto the bar's slick surface and stretched for the nearest tap.

"Young lady—" Clyde began, but he stopped short in surprise as she angled herself under the tap. Foam poured from either side of Meg's mouth and down her neck.

Baila's attention flashed to Liz. Of all her friends, she'd have the most difficulty with self-indulgence. But as Bull Whip Lizzy plucked a bottle of wine from a table-side ice bath and took an audible swig, Baila grinned.

Emilia knew her role, but Gordon didn't see it coming. He jumped back with a look of surprise when Emilia met him chest-to-chest.

Distraction. Accomplished.

And now it was her turn. Baila's stomach knotted when she marched to Asher's table and she swallowed to steady her voice. "So... is this what you do for fun?" She panned the crowd with an impassive eye, and tried to ignore the gathering of onlookers.

"Among other things." Asher's voice remained level, but his line of sight shifted from his glass to the juncture between her legs. A rush of heat crept up her neck, when his dark gleam crawled the length of her body to meet her eyes. They both knew all about those "other things."

The man next to Asher wobbled to his feet. "Would you like a chair, my dear?"

"She has one." Asher jerked his chin to her vacant table across the room then raised the glass to his lips. "I suggest you find it."

"Chair and I are well acquainted. I'm making new friends now," she said.

"How about the dance floor, then?" The man persisted.

Asher dealt the man a look that had him shrinking back into his chair.

Baila scrunched her nose at the man. "He's just jealous. Bad memory, you know. Forgot how to pick up girls."

She tipped her gaze to the rafters in thought. "As far as dancing goes—I would, but you know, the beat's all wrong for me." She reached for Asher's glass. She expected his grip to tighten, but the glass, slicked with condensation, slipped from his hand.

The ice clinked against her teeth as she tossed back the liquid. Tiny ice crystals prickled down her throat, and a chill splashed into her stomach. She tried to breathe through the rush of mint vapors that flooded her sinuses. What was this? Liquid nitrogen? Tears brimmed, and she swallowed again.

Don't cough...Do. Not. Cough. Suck it up, girl.

She blew out a chilled breath.

The drink took effect faster than she thought possible. It coated her thoughts and lulled the constant throb in her brain. Handy, but a shot that powerful on an empty belly? Oh, she'd hate herself tomorrow.

The weight of Asher's hand closed around her wrist and warmth danced up her arm. "Baila—"

She jerked away, ignoring the note of concern that had trailed after her name. He didn't *actually care* about her wellbeing, did he? "I can take a drink." She snatched a second one from the approaching waiter.

"Can you, now?"

She sucked in a breath of courage before the second blast of icy liquid hit the back of her throat. She forced it down with a single gulp that fought its entire descent.

He gave her a weary look. "That's not meant for humans."

"Really," She wheezed. "I kind-a like it." She flicked out her tongue to catch a tingling bead of liquid on her lip.

Asher's eyes narrowed on her mouth. "You have any idea how stupid that was?"

Baila's voice sounded thick to her own ears. "Nope. But I'm about to find out."

She hoped the two shots dimmed her aura enough. One more and she'd wheelbarrow nose first across the floor. She searched for Emilia's confirmation, but her sister looked too far gone to make the assessment.

The little hussy stood just a breath away from sucking face with Gordon, and this time, he seemed to rather enjoy being victimized. Good diversion on both sides, unfortunately. And Emilia's timing couldn't be worse. Strike two for the absentminded psychic.

Baila drew a breath and poised to blow a high-pitched whistle for Emilia, when the room erupted.

A heavy urban beat thundered through the speaker system, and Baila jerked her attention to the bandstand.

The players lowered their instruments and looked to one another with bewilderment.

Liz offered a beaming smile from her position near the microphone. She waved at Baila with her iPod cradled in her palm. Gordon must not have been kidding when he said necessities were easily obtainable. State of the art sound equipment must have been one of them.

"Baila! Over here," Meg called from her perch on

the bar.

Baila looked back to Asher with an impish grin. "Let's see how you handle this, shall we?"

The gathering of unfriendlies stretched to a thousand as she took Meg's hand and climbed up the bar. Her legs wobbled. The crowd tipped and the bar rolled beneath her. She pitched her body to one side, fighting for balance.

"Careful there, Tipsy." Meg steadied Baila's shoulders and pulled her close. "If we fall, at least we'll go down together." She dipped and swayed to the music and wrapped a slender arm around Baila's waist.

Baila's spine went rigid. So many rungs above her comfort level. But that's what she got for having a friskier-than-average friend.

Hisses and low mutters filtered through the crowd, and grew to rival the driving beat.

She steeled herself from the urge to dive under a nearby table, and wrapped her arms around Meg's neck.

"Oh, baby!" Meg swooned.

Heat scalded Baila's cheeks. "Not helping," she bit out.

"Baila." Charlie tugged on the hem of her dress. "Get down." He cast a helpless glance to his twin.

Clyde dropped his arms to his sides and made a slow pivot from his podium. The initial shock written on his face replaced with murderous intent. He vaulted himself over the orchestra pit and marched for the sound system, where Liz stood. She backed away with palms raised. The iPod still cradled in her hand.

Gordon and Clyde met Liz at the same time. Clyde tore at the wires, Gordon stole Liz off her feet, and the music snapped off with a metallic shriek. The crowd shuffled and watched with anxious murmurs.

Liz kicked and struggled in Gordon's arms. "Lemme go!"

Heavy steps hammered against the dance floor, and Harvey's voice rang over the commotion. "Charlie. Door. I'll take this."

"There. That's our chance," Meg whispered. She jumped down and aimed for the entrance with her upper body angled to one side, she ping-ponged through tables and chairs, hips and elbows leveraging through the crowd.

Emilia moved faster. She caught Meg's arm and tugged her closer to freedom.

Two down, but what about Liz? Baila stretched up on her toes and craned her neck in search of her friend.

Gordon and Clyde eclipsed her from view as they dragged her down the hall.

Harvey wasn't far behind them.

Liz was outnumbered with no chance to flee.

Her heart crumpled. The first escape from the gateway had already come at the price of her friends once. She wouldn't let Liz pay her way again.

Baila jumped down from the bar, and staggered into Asher's chest. His broad profile shifted to block her path. "Don't. You'll only make it worse for her."

She caught a narrow glimpse of Harvey through the crowd as he looped the cord from his neck. With a swing of his arm, Liz's cries cut short.

Panic squeezed Baila throat. No. She tried to shove past Asher but he hooked her arm in a punishing grip.

"*No!*" She spun and slammed her elbow into his midsection with all her strength.

His abs clenched and shoulders hunched forward as

he expelled a soft grunt.

Sharp gasps from the crowd told Baila her golden hour in Asher's favor had just met its end. She didn't dare face the anger that fueled in those dark eyes. She could feel it growing as his posture straightened.

Make that a thousand-and-one unfriendlies.

She darted through the peacock-hued crowd before he could grab her again.

Charlie shouted from the front door. "We've got a breach."

A half-dozen clouded figures poured through the entryway. They rushed through the mass of people. Given their appearance, their steps should've seemed weightless, but the heavy gallop of unlaced sneakers pounded the floor. They turned one direction, then veered in another, like a heard of deer caught in a department store. Not sure where to turn, but desperate for escape.

Tables jostled and chairs overturned with shattering glass. Terror erupted through the crowd with high-pitched squeals and bellowed curses. The dance floor opened as patrons shoved each other to the perimeter. Baila dug in her heels to keep from crashing into one of the passing intruders.

"Keep the repeaters separate!" Asher bellowed. "Don't let them unite."

The pale apparition paused at the urgency in Asher's voice. It turned to Baila.

A moment of hopeful recognition flickered in his wide, clouded eyes. He blinked and reached out, his voice raspy. "Muh—Marcy...Where've you been?"

Baila stepped out of reach.

He continued, unhindered. "You know, I forgot

how…bright and…pretty you are."

Baila stumbled back on an overturned chair. Her attention flashed to the man pursuing her as she attempted to scoot free. Did she know him? He dressed like he belonged here, with suspenders and riding cap all coated dusky gray. But the shoes and the shaggy hair cut...Something about him wasn't right.

He stepped closer, and his waxy lips curved to a frown. "You're late. You said you'd be home after work but—but you didn't come home."

She expected him to swipe through her like vapor, but his icy grip solidified and stung her forearm on contact. Baila jerked away and shook her head. "I'm not Marcy." She wanted to explain further, but that far-away look in his eye told her she'd never reach him.

His face contorted. "Marcy, please." He hooked icy claws in the front of her dress and dragged her forward like a rag doll.

Asher charged between them, leading with his shoulder, and knocked the man to the floor. The man's head smacked the ground with a wet thud, but the blow didn't seem to register. Greed flashed in his eyes. Words rushed out in desperation as he crawled after Baila. "Where've you been, huh? Where've you been?" His voice grew louder.

Asher pulled the man back by his throat with enough force to send him flying through the air. He slammed against the wall. The man's head lolled to one side and plaster rained onto his shaggy, gray mop.

Asher nearly pulled Baila's arm from its socket when he wrenched it behind her back.

"Charlie, secure this room." He shoved Baila for the same hall Liz had taken, to the first door on the right. When the door flung open and slammed against its adjoining wall, Gordon, Clyde, and Harvey all turned. Liz greeted her with a fearful look and massaged the angry rash at her throat.

"We don't need three of you. Harvey, take your girl. The rest, get out," Asher said.

Outside the door, the band resumed a pretty decent imitation of the rolling beat Liz had played, whether in parity or encouragement, Baila wasn't sure, but it seemed to only heighten Clyde's rage. "Who's responsible for this? Which one?" he demanded.

Liz's faun-colored eyes hardened with determination when her gaze found Baila.

Clyde started for Liz, hands reaching for her throat.

Baila's panic spiked, and she lurched forward to block his path. "I am," she cried. "It's me."

In one step Clyde rounded on her. He grabbed her by the shoulders and threw her into the desk. Her diaphragm seized on impact, and her hands skated over a mass of papers as she fought to right herself. Clyde rammed the heel of his hand between her shoulder blades and held her in place.

He ripped her zipper down the back of her dress and her blood turned to ice.

Oh god...

Cool air brushed the full length of her back. She turned her head, paper crumpled under her cheek as she watched Clyde struggle with his shirt.

Oh god, oh god...

Asher's voice boomed through the cluttered office. "I said out!"

The weight between her shoulders lifted when Clyde stepped away. But her upper body mashed to the littered surface again as Asher took his place.

"Look who's finally decided to do his fucking job," Clyde sneered. "And by god, you'd better, 'cause I'm not going to let you lose this for us."

Baila met the cold malice in Asher's eyes and her hope went limp. Oh, he'd do it all right. Whatever "it" was.

Asher loosened his shirt, tugged his amulet free, and slipped it into his pocket. With a flick of his wrist the remaining cord grew thick and long.

Oh. That.

Asher nodded to his men. "Clyde, give your brother some help out there. Harvey, find another room. Gordon? Locate the others."

Baila choked back a sob of fear at the long look Gordon gave her, like a misbegotten angel stripped of his mercy. He turned his back, and the room opened to the chaos outside. Harvey dragged Liz to the door. Her voice turned shrill. "Don't hurt her. You can't!"

Harvey chuckled. "Oh, honey, you'll get your fair share."

"Let her go. You don't understand," Liz persisted.

"Shut the door, Harvey," Asher said.

The room muted again as the door clicked shut and her own anxious pants filled her ears.

He jerked the dress from her shoulders and stretched the zipper wide.

"Why?" he demanded. He unhooked her bra and the material slipped away. She tried to jerk upright, but he shoved her down again. "Why did you test me?"

A cool hand smoothed down her back and raised goose bumps over her skin.

"Don't. Move." Asher's touch disappeared as he

took a step back.

She held her breath and waited for the sound of his whip to cut through the air, through the echo of Gordon's voice murmuring over the sound system outside. "Ladies and gentlemen, we apologize for the inconvenience—"

Crack.

A scream tore from Baila's throat, and her knees buckled. She clung to the bulky desk expecting a flash of searing pain.

But nothing came. It hadn't touched her.

"Again," he demanded.

Her voice came at a near whisper through trembling lips. "Don't—"

Crack.

Cold breath met her ear with a deadly hiss. "Scream."

She whimpered and a warm tear slid down her cheek. Couldn't he just hit her already? Get this over with?

"We have no choice here, Baila. We have no choice," he said.

But he did. He could stand up to them. He could take her home. Instead he chose to punish her, just like they expected him to. Be a good little collector.

Crack.

She clenched her jaw.

His hand smoothed up her thigh, pushing her dress up with it. "If you don't start making some noise..." His palm smacked the round curve of her ass.

Baila cried out and tried to wrench herself free.

He leaned his forearm into her back to prevent her twisting away. Soft, languid circles played over her stinging flesh until only the feel of his touch remained. The hard edge in his voice softened. "Is that what it takes? You want that?"

Humiliation. That's what he wanted, long, and harsh, and loud enough for the patrons outside to hear. He wanted to make an example of her, but Baila wasn't about to make it easy on him. *Fear*. She reminded herself. *Not an option*.

When he smacked her again, Baila bit her cheek to hold back the cry. The sharp sting heated her skin, but it didn't hurt like the last one. Did Asher go easy? Or did her own conviction dull the pain? She wasn't sure, but she'd sure as hell use it to her advantage.

Asher caressed her skin again, as if trying to undo the pain he'd caused. Baila wouldn't have it. She'd make him own it. She pushed her backside into his hand and sucked in a long breath, ready for the next strike.

His hand stilled and an eternity seemed to pass in the sound-dampened room.

He struck her again, not harder, but louder this time. As if he'd cupped his hand just slightly, adjusting for minimum pain, maximum noise. He didn't want to hurt her. He just wanted her to play the game.

He wanted noise? She'd give him noise.

She'd play, all right.

Baila forced out a deep moan. It came shakier than she expected, but it seemed to do the trick.

"Damn, Baila—" He shifted directly behind her and covered her bare skin with his body. His mouth closed over the nape of her neck, and teeth scraped along her skin. "You're asking for it again."

Was she ever. She rocked her backside against him

in agreement.

His breath hitched against her, and he tugged her tight to his chest.

Her dress slipped down to puddle around her waist as Asher cupped her breasts with both hands. Baila reached back and laced her fingers through his hair. Oh, what she wouldn't give to have that mouth on her again.

When his thumbs grazed over her nipples, Baila released a breathy moan—a real moan this time, and Asher seemed to know the difference. He plucked at her nipples until they formed tight aching buds, then released them.

He chuckled at her groan of frustration.

"That's good, doll, but not what I'm looking for. You can do better than that." He urged her to the desk again.

Her forehead thunked against the wood. Not the spanking thing again. That's not what she wanted. She wanted...

Oh.

Oh, my...

A sweet caress over her wounded territory turned dangerous, when he pulled her lacy thong to one side. "There are some things I remember quite well..." His hand followed the crevice of her bottom to the moist heat between her legs. She bucked forward, and her back arched with a streak of fear. The sound that escaped her was more pleading than pained.

"Better," he said in encouragement.

Baila's thoughts disintegrated when he pushed a finger past her moist folds. Her mouth dropped open with a mix of wonder and surprise.

Asher sucked a breath through clenched teeth. "So hot." His finger reached in to massage her throbbing core. The languid circles coaxed a power from Baila that seemed beyond her control. Her moment of hesitation fled, and she rocked her hips against his hand. Her tiny cries grew urgent.

His voice rumbled at the hollow between her shoulders. "More. I want more."

Take it, for god's sake, take it! Just don't ever let this end.

His hand retreated, but before she could protest, his slick fingers rubbed over her throbbing clit. Her nails dug into the polished wood and she shuddered against each writhing stroke.

The metal grate of his zipper sounded behind her and his motion grew distracted with the sound of ruffled clothes.

After two ragged breaths, his hand found its rhythm again and the hard length of his penis caressed her inner thigh. Her muscles clenched tight, and her breathing stilled.

He must have recognized her hesitation, because his fingers slowed and the smooth stroke of his penis on her inner thigh continued without advance.

"Touch it, feel it," he said.

She paused, and he asked her again.

She reached a trembling hand between her thighs to brush the silky tip. He nudged her palm to open and glided himself in and out of her hand. Large enough to do damage, she knew that much, but the texture and warmth of him promised something more.

An offering of sorts, because that potential for damage now lie in Baila's hands. A simple yank or twist could bring him to his knees in a hurry. But what would hurting him buy her? Staying on Asher's good side could be so much more rewarding.

"I'm not going to hurt you—" His words cut short as Baila angled him to stroke along the heated folds between her legs. Her knees grew weak, and she pressed closer to him. Only her tendon-aching grip on the desk kept her off the floor.

Asher bent down slightly and positioned himself at her opening. She inched forward again in a moment's hesitation, but couldn't get far with that damn desk in the way.

He pushed and stretched against her until she felt sure she would tear.

He eased back.

She wanted to tell him to stop there, but he thrust forward again and she took him in completely. The scream she released echoed repeatedly through the room.

No...She was still screaming. That raspy cry of demand sounded foreign to her own ears, and it increased with the velocity of each thrust until she tipped over the crest of her orgasm.

"I'm sorry," Asher whispered in her ear, when his driving beat only increased its urgency. The desk scooted across the floor with a sharp squeak. His arms squeezed tight around her, and his whole body grew tense. That's when the pull came again.

Warmth peeled away from her body with shocking speed until only ice remained. Despite the force of every thrust Asher dealt her, she curled her back to the blistering heat of his chest, desperate to soak up the warmth he'd stolen. The feeling in her hands and feet tingled away when Asher finally roared in triumph.

The moment his skin lost contact with hers, her grip on the desk gave way. The weakness that consumed her felt more powerful than any chemical she'd known—and Baila had met some pretty wicked chemicals in her day.

No, this was all Asher.

Anyone with an ounce of conviction would have socked him right in the nads for all he'd taken from her, but Baila felt no conviction. Only fear.

Not fear of Asher himself, but the familiar erosion of life—of control. The same loss that courted her from the hospital bed years ago. The one that waited, even now, with its boney finger poised on her doorbell.

Her mind and body suspended in a tide pool without the strength to fight its current on the edge of being sucked into darkness. She'd known that feeling often enough, and recognized it for the brink that it was.

If she blacked out, would she ever wake back up?

He caught her before she hit the floor and swung her into his arms, but still the fear of slipping into unconsciousness consumed her. She clung to his chest and squeezed her legs tight over his arm.

He settled onto a black leather couch and pulled his shirt around her.

The shivering...she couldn't make it stop. Her muscles ached from the constant spasms to produce heat, but the only warmth in the room came from him. She couldn't explain it, but for some reason she couldn't draw on it.

Baila closed her eyes and tried to will the cold ache away.

Her escape, the giant mess she'd just made,

everything fell secondary to the desperate urge to warm herself. To stay alive.

He held her there, silent for what seemed like hours, until a heavy fist pounded on the door.

"Hey, Asher. Company."

Chapter Nine

"Stay here." As if the command was even necessary. After what he'd done, he doubted she'd be going anywhere. He shifted Baila to the heated corner of the couch where he'd sat and tucked his shirt around her.

Couch. That would've been nice. Real gentlemanly. As opposed to the sharp, unforgiving edge of the desk. Baila said it right, he was a bastard.

Not that Baila had complained.

Then again, she wouldn't, would she.

She had been strong, all right, but Asher hadn't counted on the power of his own urge to take her. Now look where they'd landed. A one-man-boiler-room and a babe-cicle. He wiped the sweat from his brow. On a regular day, this predicament wouldn't trouble him. He'd cool down eventually and Baila would return to her bratty ol' self in no time.

Baila dipped her head, tucking the bluish tip of her nose under the shirt's collar.

No time at all—give or take a month.

He jerked the door open to find Lilith with her hip cocked. If he slammed the door hard enough, he might be able to pancake her face. That thought alone made his lips stretch to match her smarmy expression.

"I heard about the breech—" Her gaze dropped to his toes and sprung back again. She arched a raven eyebrow. "Well, don't you look...refreshed?"

"The breech was minor. It's taken care of." He braced one arm on the doorframe to block her. "Question is, why were the repeaters so close to Saltair tonight? A little convenient, don't you think?"

"I'm not here to contemplate mindless repeaters. I *am* asking, however, what you've been up to instead of managing your clients. Alex gave you Saltair in hopes you'd learn to appreciate an honorable career. A more elite class of people."

"What are you saying, Lilith? Those muscle-bound textile boys aren't good enough for polite society? They're good enough for you..."

Her mouth dropped open in a how-did-you-know gasp of offense.

Who didn't know?

Her expression flashed to anger, and she ducked under his arm. Asher clenched his fist and compressed the urge to yank her back out by the hair.

She panned the room until she found Baila's huddled figure. "Aaand now I have my answer. Well done, Asher. Looks like you've managed to singlehandedly drain your first whore. Not an easy feat—"

"She's not a whore."

"She is now." Lilith's attention veered to the doorway and her face lit up like Christmas. Only two things inspired that kind of delight in his step-mother, supreme authority, and nailing Asher's ass to the wall.

"—what's the meaning if this?" his father asked, strolling in.

Asher looked skyward. Great. A two-for-one. "Again. Convenient."

Lilith's grin grew more shark-toothed by the second. "Your darling son inherited the Landon family appetite. I told you this was a mistake. Look what he's done to her."

Asher's father stalked forward and tugged the cloth that eclipsed Baila's face. She kept her eyes squeezed shut, thank god. The pain flickering over her features was message enough. To see it ten-fold in her eyes would only make his chest ache more.

Why then, did he silently will them to open? To watch them scan the room until she found him? Recognized him.

His father flung the cloth back in place. "My reputation's on the line here."

Asher fought back a snort. Self-imposed reputations are a little tough to mar. Did he really believe the community didn't know about the mayor's dirty appetite either? Who was he dealing with tonight? Mayor Obtuse and Just Plain Stupid?

"She acted up. I responded," Asher said.

"I'll say," Lilith replied.

That retort seemed to suck back into her mouth at the dangerous look Asher narrowed on her. She took a step back. "Look, these women weren't meant for this world. Bringing them down here ripe for the slaughter won't sit well with polite society. You need to hand them over where they can be sedated and safely harvested. What you did here was unconscionable."

And didn't he know it. But there wasn't a sorry in the world big enough to undo it. He squared his shoulders. "This was a trial run, and you of all people know it worked. You can't deny the outpouring of people we had tonight—even after the breech—and tomorrow will be even bigger. If these women simply behave..." He shrugged. "Where's the fun in that?"

"You're trying to tell me you planned this?" His father asked.

He stared unblinking. Of course he hadn't planned this. He hadn't planned to ruin Baila like this.

And not only her aura.

His gaze itched to return to the trembling ball on the couch, but he couldn't look. Not now. He remembered the way she felt when he slipped inside her—not only hot, the girl was tight. It had been quite a while for her—if ever.

A sick feeling churned in his gut, but being the *bastard* that he was, he'd take the credit for all of it. He nodded.

His father's shoulders relaxed. "Well, you can't go doing that every night. You'll run out of girls."

Asher hoped the gaze he shot Baila looked impassive. "She's strong enough. She'll recover."

Another lie. He knew what lay inside her. He'd tasted it the first time they met. But now. Now it was undeniable. The aftertaste of chilled orchids seemed to permeate his skin and perfume the air around him so intimately that only he could detect it.

He hadn't ever experienced it before—hell, he didn't even know what chilled orchids tasted like, but he'd heard it often enough to recognize the sign. Baila had the mark of death growing inside her.

His father shook his head. "I don't know why I even bother giving you more time."

Of course you do. You want a shot at getting one too. A ripe, young earth-bound angel to soil and enslave. Anger sizzled in Asher's veins. The thought of scoring a hellcat human and forcing her to conform got his father all stupid inside.

"I'll give you three days to get this one back in working order, else she'll have to go to the boarding house to convalesce," his father said.

Asher frowned. "You mean die."

Lilith's eyes narrowed. "Are you calling me a murderer?"

Not out loud, but yes. Everyone in the room knew her practice was less than honest.

Just like the cheap stunt with herding those repeaters into his dance hall. They never came that close to town unless they were following human aura. Asher's girls were all accounted for—well, until Meg and Emilia escaped, but who better to supply the trail then the one with the all-powerful amulet.

His father breathed a sigh of defeat. "You won't get any more chances. If you can't contain them without sedating or destroying them, they have no place here. You can't go off ruining people like this when you get into power."

"Never stopped you," Lilith sneered under her breath.

Alex paused and he turned on Lilith with banked rage in his voice. "You're crossing a line, woman."

Lilith squared her shoulders. A huge feat considering Alex looked like he was ready to tear her to pieces. Asher almost felt sorry for her. The minute she became full of herself his father always felt the need to knock her down a peg or two.

Asher often wondered if he wouldn't have done the same if he and his father's roles were reversed. He thrust the idea from his mind. No, Lilith would be detestable even if she weren't his stepmother. He looked to Baila. But he seemed to become more and more like Alex every day.

The thought fueled the disgust inside him. This place needed a leader. Not an abuser. He didn't want to be either of those things.

****

Blinding pain spanned the confines of her skull and seared brighter with every sound. She buried her head under the musty pillow they'd issued her, but even the sound of her own breath seemed more than she could stand.

Drugs. She needed drugs. And not the frivolous recreational kind, she needed the knock her down for a week kind.

"Baila..."

She scrunched her face in response.

"She's having one of those headaches again," Liz whispered.

But who was she whispering to? Despite the pain, Baila's ears perked for the response, praying that only a female voice responded.

"Where's Gordon with that bag?"

Asher. Her heart rate chimed pain through her ears and rang out the sound of his soft mummers.

What had he said? Something about the bag. Hopefully the one she'd dropped as she crossed the portal. It had her medicine in it. Her thoughts pinned on that tiny brown bottle. But...but how did he *know* she needed that? The drink she had last night wasn't meant for human consumption. Could she still cry hangover? Or had Liz betrayed her secret?

Hasty footsteps knocked at her skull until a waterlogged bag slapped the floor beside her. A soft moan slipped between her lips. She eased her fisted grip on the pillow and peered out through bleary, narrow slits.

Asher crouched beside her with his glossy, dark head bowed and his jaw set with determination. He dug through the bag until he pulled out a bottle, half-filled with murky water and a layer of white sediment just visible through the sap-colored plastic.

His gaze flicked to her, and in that moment she knew. Someone had told him. Her hope sank and another wave of pain crashed over her. She squeezed her eyes shut and willed herself not to cry.

"Oh, god," Liz whispered.

No kidding. A little divine intervention would be great right now, but Baila probably wouldn't find any here. The local population didn't seem too keen on finding peace with their maker. More of an uneasy truce.

If she died here...she'd never rest.

Asher pushed out a heavy sigh and tossed the bottle back. "Where is it?"

A long pause stretched through the room.

"The cancer. Where is it?" He demanded.

Baila held her breath and stole another glance to Liz.

Liz's voice cracked. "I don't know. I saw the CAT scan once, but it could've been one of those..."—she made a vague, conjuring gesture with her hands— "those ink blot tests thingies for all I know. It's in her head."

"I can't just search through her entire brain looking for it. It's going to be painful enough as is," he growled.

Her stomach churned. He wanted inside her head?

He couldn't be trained for that. The man dealt in dead people, and harvesting live people until they *became* dead people. She'd seen every holistic healer, shaman, and oncology specialist worth the money. None of them could save her. What made him so special?

Asher stared at her, his expression unreadable. "Out of the room. Everyone."

Baila curled her head deeper into the pillow. Good idea. That would be the humane option. No more sound. No more loved ones to watch her suffer.

"Baila?" Liz whispered.

She didn't respond.

"I didn't tell him, if that's what you think. Somehow he knew." The honesty in Liz's voice seemed clear. She paused. "I think he really wants to help you."

The shuffle of footsteps fell away from the room, but she knew Asher hadn't left. She could feel him, sense his gaze boring through her pillow.

She tightened her grip against Asher's gradual pull on her floppy, feather-down shield, but the force only increased until her hands slipped from the pillowcase.

"Baila—"

She pushed out a frustrated breath. Why wouldn't he just go away?

"Tell me where it is."

Her cracked lips parted with a barely audible whisper. "Where's what?"

He canted his head. "You think after existing down here all these years, I don't know what death tastes like?"

If she had the energy she'd slap him. To call someone a bad kisser was one thing, but to say they tasted like death? Her fists tightened on the pillow and she strained to pull it back over her head, but she couldn't overpower him. Large warm hands soothed over her fists and unhooked the pillow from her grip. He tossed it away. "I think you'd taste much better without it."

Her diaphragm seized in a restrained sob. Is that all he wanted—to improve her flavor for all the monsters waiting to feast on her? She'd rather die here, a bedraggled, anemic mess.

But her friends, she couldn't just leave them, and she couldn't let them watch her die like this. She should get swallowed whole by a shark or disappear over Niagara Falls. Something quick and fitting. Not this. A warm tear slipped from between her lashes.

Asher cupped her cheek and brushed the tears with the pad of his thumb. Warm tingles traced over her skin.

"I know what you're thinking."

Oh really? *Did his captives often sock him in the face?*

"With as much as I really do love the stubbornness, you conjured me. You wanted something. Admit it or not. At least take what I can offer you." He looked away. "I've already taken more than my fair share."

Did he really just pull out the L-word? A hollow moment of silence shouldn't hold enough power to crumble her walls.

It hit with sledgehammer force.

How could someone she knew so little about, move her so easily? Would he have affected her like this in her own world? On her terms?

The first kiss he dealt her had been on solid ground, and it still sent her body reeling. How could a mere ghost—the fading image of what once was, still hold so much power over her?

"Asher?" The sound of his name caught tight in her throat. She swallowed back the emotion and started again. "How did you die?"

A brief pause stretched between them.

Asher expelled a troubled sigh. "Too long ago to remember. This place has a way of dragging your memories away if you don't take care of them. I guess that event wasn't one I especially cared for. Not that it matters. If I hadn't died, I never would have met you."

"Now tell me where." He persisted.

Oh...hell. She used her palm to cover a baseball-sized area just behind her ear. "Here." She slid her hand back, to the base of her skull. "And...here."

He sat back. Tension knotted his brows.

"The more it's spread and the finer its fingers, the longer it will take to get rid of it."

She squeezed her eyes closed and shook her head. "Impossible."

But Asher ignored her. "I can't do it by hand without killing you. We have to sedate."

"Not that stupid whip again..."

He shook his head slow, regretful. "Have to go deeper than that."

How much deeper than near-dead did she have to go? Another tear slipped down. She'd had enough wistful thinking. Time to face reality.

His eyes grew tender. "You scared?"

Scared? She bit her lip. Fear wasn't an option. Not now, not ever. But if this wasn't fear, then fear had grown an evil twin. She was petrified.

He leaned forward and brushed his soft lips over

her forehead. "I'll take good care of you. Promise."

"Don't want you to," she said.

"You have no choice." He got to his feet. "Neither do I."

Chapter Ten

Hot tension knotted in his shoulders a hundred yards before he met the parasitic building that had molded onto the Saltair's south face.

He could already hear it.

A mix of swanky jazz tunes laced over one another and filtered from every window in an indistinguishable racket. The pop and crackle of the sound system only added to the thrash of the shuffling crowd around him. But the quality of the music didn't matter. It wasn't meant to lure in customers, it was meant to drown out the sound from within.

A hundred or more of purgatory's upper and middle class made their way beyond the strewn lights of the Saltair resort's north side. A fine, gray dust spiraled in their wake and itched in Asher's lungs.

The boarding house wasn't open for the evening, but the crowd had already funneled to a knot-and-tapered line that snaked from the building's paint-caked south porch. The crowd's jovial chatter quieted the closer they came, and their thirsty gazes fixed straight ahead, as if minding a sacred oath to forget who they'd seen here and why they'd come.

Asher would wager that no thought of their victims ever fell into the equation. No man that came this far, ever left without getting his fill. If there were even a mediocre battle of ethics, the girls had lost every time.

Given another option their fate might be different, but this was it. Siphon aura from the living, or lose every memory you've known.

"First fifteen to level three," Lilith's main assistant called from the door, her silhouette but a thin line lurking in the entryway's shadow.

An eruption of grating windows split through the music. A flurry of moths sprang from the open panes, shooed by pale feminine hands and tattered clothes. A feeble attempt at putting on airs for the customers. The moths spiraled and dove until they found new purchase on the building's facade. The closer he got, the thicker the winged nuisances became. They fanned at his face and chased along his back. Swatting them away became useless in a hurry. He panned the insect-cloaked line ahead of him. At least he didn't have to worry about being recognized.

When the first group entered, the crowd shifted up the line. It created just enough distraction for Asher to slip beyond the main entrance and along the building's exterior wall. The salmon paint and ruby shutters faded as he rounded the corner, exposing gray, riddled wood and protruding nails, like the ugly side of a two-faced mask. The music dampened a bit but it still filtered through gaps in the building, but the tension in his shoulders didn't ease.

With a steady push of energy at his feet, he lifted just inches from the crawling mist and decaying branches that guarded this side of the building. The boarding house was a five-story-tall wart that had fixed itself to the Saltair's three-mile-long south wall. This far out, use of power became more guideline than law. Not that anyone hung around to police it—they were too afraid of the repeaters haunting the bog.

The hum of crickets fell silent as he approached the haggard back porch that sagged in the middle and grinned with gapped, broken rails.

Before his foot met the first step, he spotted them. Two repeaters just beyond the lawn's reach. They stumbled over uneven ground, murmuring and picking their way through garbage and tattered clothing.

Asher felt his chest where the amulet lay hidden, and with a deep intake of breath, he used it to compact Baila's pilfered aura down into the depths of his core. He couldn't let the repeaters find it. If they found a hint of her inside him, he'd never be able to shake them.

Repeaters only knew two things: confusion and anger. By themselves, these two weren't a threat, but together, their potential for violence made them pretty effective predators. Unlike the civil, amulet-toting members of Saltair, these apparitions never got full. Without the amulet's power, and without replenishment, their minds had gone. They couldn't retain an aura anymore. Couldn't remember how. But they'd siphon an entire army if they could.

Asher wouldn't give them the chance tonight. He'd slink in and collect the sedative before they could even detect him. He may not be the most ethical man, but he knew his profession. Collecting would always be it. No matter what political position this town tried to cram down his throat.

The two repeaters were permitted here for a reason. As coincidental guardians, they were meant to protect the profit here, not the people. He'd seen them here before. Lilith kept them around by offering "scraps", unfortunate patrons that couldn't settle their debt. She'd tie them to what she called "the spindle tree", a gnarled, tree-like statue that had been painted black, and let the repeaters do their deed. Yes, fair Lilith was a mobster if there ever was one—a Sheba with shark's teeth. She had no need to guard the sedative she used on her girls.

Not until now.

He guessed the notion still hadn't crossed her withering mind.

Asher pulled back from his thoughts when the two ghosts bumped into each other and staggered back in shock. As if yanked into a new and unfamiliar world, their faces filled with wonder. They angled their heads in unison, evaluating each other's purpose, weighing each other's benefit. They circled until they fell in step together with apparently one destination in mind.

With all that aura pulsing inside the building it wasn't surprising when they turned his way. Wasn't ideal, but it wasn't surprising.

A little vanishing act would've made the job easier, but this wasn't earth and the rules were different here. In purgatory, he couldn't shift from a solid form into a mist or a puff of moths as it were. Which meant the pile of oh-shit he's just stepped in, wouldn't be so easy to shake off.

"My keys." One of the repeaters hunched over and scanned the ground. "I—I lost my keys." He shuffled to Asher's feet, and his gaze crawled to meet him with a vacant, cloudy stare. "You." His mouth flapped open and closed. The two ghosts exchanged a confused glance. "You seen my keys, friend?"

Asher stared. Mention of the keys brought the man's identity screaming back. Herbert Catcher, the boarding house's original owner. Lilith took over when the man lost his mind—or more likely, had it raped from him. Apart from running a distasteful business, the man always had a conservative air puffing from beneath his bright red suspenders.

Not anymore. The level of desperation roiling under the surface set Asher nerves on high alert.

The longer he stood there, the worse his odds became. Asher could strike first, maybe stun them, but it might draw too much attention. He forced an offhanded smile and slapped Herbert on the shoulder. "Check your pocket, ole boy."

The man jerked at Asher's touch, then something clicked in his expression. He searched from one palm to the other and replayed Asher's words under his breath. "Pocket...pocket." He looked to his partner who was busy patting his dusty overcoat. Herbert mimed the same movement with his brows furrowed and uncertain.

Asher sidestepped closer to the porch.

A woman's cry filtered out from the house. It seemed to hold more anger and determination than a sedated girl would be capable of. And it sounded familiar.

It snapped Herbert to attention.

Asher froze. He shifted his weight to the balls of his feet, ready to strike at the first hint of opposition.

Herbert's toothless grin spread wide and he waved a thank you with the key ring looped around his middle finger, the keys dangling in his palm.

But the expression didn't last.

The furious cry sounded again, louder this time. Asher flicked an irritated glance to the torn screen door.

Herbert's chalky lips drooped to a frown, and he felt his pockets again. "My keys...No, these aren't my keys." His face twisted in rage. "You stole them, didn't you?" He looked to his friend in an apparent bid for support. "He stole my keys!"

That's all it took. Both specters advanced as one with their heads down like twin battering rams.

Asher jumped to one side to avoid the blow. For as ancient as they were, they moved quickly. The second man staggered over the front steps and into the wall, but Harold got lucky. He caught a thick arm around Asher's waist and pulled himself away from the forward momentum.

The pain of Harold's touch came in an instant, a searing cold that permeated to the bone. With a roar, Asher slammed his elbow to the top of Harold's head with enough force to stun him.

The man let go.

The moment Harold slipped to the dirt, his partner came back for more. He crashed into Asher's chest.

Cold spines of pain gripped his heart as the force knocked him on his back.

He took the partner to the ground with him, and hurled the man over his head with a push of his feet.

The man crashed into a lone, blackened tree.

The force sent debris in every direction.

Asher jackknifed upright as the other man charged him. Asher's skull cracked against the ground again. Frozen hands squeezed his throat. "Where are they? *Where are they*?" Harold growled through clenched jowls.

Asher's fist whistled through the air, missing its target as Harold ducked away. The world around him began to float in a watery haze.

Harold's gaze dipped and caught at the hollow of

Asher's throat. His eyes grew wide. The man eased his grip and reached for the chain that had slipped from the white, silk shirt.

Harold's hands released him altogether as he tugged hand over hand to reveal the full length of his amulet's chain.

Asher balled his fist and swung again. This time his punch connected.

The man's head snapped to one side and he expelled a muffled cry, but his legs still wrapped around Asher's midsection, his touch draining precious strength and aura by the second.

Asher rolled to one side and shoved the man away.

Harold didn't waste time getting to his feet, and he quick-crawled back to the fight.

Asher spun around and struck out with a kick. His heel hit Harold's jaw with a thick pop. Harold dropped to the ground. This time he didn't get up.

The clearing grew quiet, and the muffled tunes filtered back in. Asher waited for the telltale shriek of the screen door, but after a few tense seconds, nothing came.

Slipping inside, the smell hit him next. The sharp scent of cleanser hung so pungent in the kitchen, it burned his sinuses. Just one more token of Lilith's demand for order and control.

He blinked to clear his vision and found the outline of the basement door. Its padlock unhinged. Lilith stored the sedative where she did all her "prep" work, and she shelved enough to knock out Earth's entire Salt Lake metropolitan area.

With the lock hanging free, Asher knew that stealing the sedative had just become more difficult.

The screams hadn't come from the floors above. Lilith, or one of her assistants, was down there.

Prepping someone right now.

Chapter Eleven

No collectors had gone scavenging since he and the boys had returned. And if someone tried, they couldn't make it to earth and back so quickly. Whoever they were working on, they had found right here in town.

Meg. Emilia. They'd escaped last night under the chaos and haven't been found yet.

With a small push of energy, he floated down the stairs. Lilith had done some redecorating since he'd been here. A maze of blue, cast-iron barrels were stacked nine-feet-high through the basement. How Lilith managed to obtain them from the mill, or what they contained, he didn't know.

But Harvey would.

The man was a good collector, but when the day job called, he kept it to himself. A big man has a lot of room for carrying secrets, and the more Asher learned about Harvey and his association with Lilith, the less he liked him.

The harsh gurgling sound met his ears the moment he cleared the stairwell. He knew what it meant. He wound a path through rust-streaked cerulean pillars. Not the most sanitary of conditions, especially for Lilith. He touched the liquid that wept from one barrel and rubbed it between his thumb and forefinger.

Silk worms. He'd know that musky-sweet scent anywhere. The worms in purgatory were a voracious breed, kept in barrels just like these. They'd eat just about anything, live anywhere. The mill bred them to supply purgatory with all its material needs. Not to mention the edible ones. No wonder everything here tasted like shit. But what were they doing here?

The panicked gurgle sound yanked his attention to the prep area at the far corner of the basement.

"Hurry up." One of Lilith's assistants said.

"—if you'd keep her still," demanded the other.

"—I'm trying. The stupid straps are coming loose."

Asher could just make out Meg's pixie-like frame. Lit by a single, dangling light bulb, she was webbed to the ceramic table by two spindly women. One straddled her chest and held a funnel tight to her face. The other stretched to hold her legs. A wet gurgle echoed through the funnel, and milky liquid rolled from Meg's nose. Her eyes squeezed tight.

"Drink," the woman with the funnel said.

Meg wrenched her head to one side, then the other, but made little progress. Liquid sprayed from the funnel. The woman leaning over her wiped an arm across her eyes and scowled. "Hold her nose."

The second woman sneered. "I only have two hands."

The woman's complaint cut short when Meg's back arched off the white, marble table, only to slam down again.

"Drink or breathe it, I don't care, but it's going down," the funnel woman warned.

Meg kicked at the table and a loud bang echoed though the room.

The second women scrambled to secure her. "She's getting loose—"

Another thrash from Meg's leg sent the second woman stumbling from the table and into one of the unsealed barrels behind her.

The barrel seemed to teeter in slow motion.

The woman with the funnel managed a panicked gasp just before the barrel crashed to the floor with a mighty boom. The barrel's lid popped free and rolled across the floor. A slosh of fluid and worms raced from the barrel.

"Now look what you've done," the funnel woman said. But the second woman didn't even spare a glance backward. Her scowl trained on Meg as she rushed back to the table.

Stepping behind the last barrel guarding the prep area, Asher found a slender arm stretched across the floor, palm up with its waxy fingers curled in sleep. Her body partially cast out of the overturned barrel. The tiny flicker of her aura felt unmistakable, similar to Baila's but not as vibrant.

The fattened worms sloughed away from her body. Silver-dollar-sized welts covered her skin where the worms had been. The insects had already ingested her clothes, the remnants of which could only be found under her arms and between her legs where the insects couldn't reach.

Emilia kept her teeth clenched tight. Her head twitched every so often in what seemed a feeble attempt to rid herself of the insects.

Like a record stuck on replay. As if she were already adopting the first signs of her future. To become a repeater. And she would, if Asher didn't hurry. As the slime and insects slipped away and raced for the drain, Asher heart sickened. Did Harvey lure

Meg and Emilia here? Sold them both to Lilith because if he couldn't have Meg? And what was the going rate for betrayal these days? Asher crouched and found the thready pulse at her wrist.

Out cold. She'd put up a fight though. Her lacquered nails were ragged and torn. The warm tan on Emilia's inner arm blanched with frosted, purple bruises.

He pulled away without a sound and rounded his attention to the prep table. A hollow cry echoed through the pillars.

Asher breathed an icy snarl. Come on Meg, cooperate. Stop fighting and drink.

He couldn't move in until Meg went under. The walls were too thin to risk it. And with only one way in and one out, getting caught here wasn't an option. Oh he'd enjoy pounding Lilith's minions into ground beef, but getting his girls out would take an element of surprise and more than just him.

He pulled out the cell phone Gordon had given him and thumbed a quick message to the twins.

And if Harvey thought he had balls big enough to cross him, Asher had no problem slicing them off. There might be stiff repercussions for breaking the laws of purgatory, but the collectors had a code of their own. No one ever steals from a collector. Ever.

The sedative worked fast. Already Meg's struggle wavered, and her aura glowed brighter around her—a cosmetic effect for those locals who could no longer detect the human aura.

With a collective sigh, the women released her flaccid body. Meg's bare leg dangled from the edge of the table. How could anyone take pleasure from a woman in that state? The image it brought made his stomach recoil. He'd been living on the first sip of his victims for so long he'd forgotten what the rest of his world had been feeding on.

Or maybe he hadn't forgotten, just blocked it out.

"Take her upstairs," the funnel woman said.

The second woman gestured to Emilia. "What about the mess?"

"I'm not touching that. Let the worms eat her for all I care. She'll be lighter when there's just bones anyway."

Lilith's tone carried down the stairs. "What's taking so long?"

"Now you're in for it," the second woman whispered.

The funnel clattered into the porcelain sink. "She was a fighter, Ms. Lilith."

"Well she isn't fighting now. Get her up here. Clean out room one-fourteen, you can put her there."

"—One-fourteen. That was one of the new girls," the second woman whispered. Her brow wrinkled. "She's already used up?"

"One-fourteen's for VIPs only. They have...preferences. Not that it's any of your business," Lilith said.

The girls exchanged sour looks.

Lilith expelled an exaggerated huff and the hammer of heels started down the stairs. She paused when she caught sight of Emilia, then marched forward again. "What's this mess? She isn't ready. Not even close...yet here you are, standing around like a bunch of ninnies. Get the other one draped. Get her upstairs. I'll handle...this."

"But we're out of drapes—"

"—I don't care. Find something." Lilith's attention fell to Meg's tattered, navy dress on the floor. She kicked it to the far corner of the room and turned to the funnel woman. "It doesn't matter where she came from or how she got here. She's no different from any other whore in this house. She'll dress accordingly."

"Yes, Ms. Landin," they muttered.

Seemingly satisfied with her assistant's jump to action, Lilith seemed to forget about Emilia. She wandered her garden of pillars with measured steps while her minions hauled Meg upstairs. Lilith trailed a hand along the width of the barrels in time to the music above, tapping every so often. Then she stopped and pressed an ear to the ribbed metal. A slow smile stretched across her face.

Very tempting scenario with Lilith alone and the music blaring. How much time would pass before someone missed her?

Judging from her minions, they wouldn't.

Asher stepped from the shadows and into her path. "What are you doing with my girls?"

Her gasp seemed to suck the color from her face. "They're not yours."

He nodded to Emilia. "Sure looks like mine. Possessions are kind of my thing, Lilith. I don't like to part with them. Makes me angry."

She straightened. "Then maybe you shouldn't let them to wander off."

"Maybe."

Lilith spoke slowly. "But if you'd like to make a trade..."

"Don't need to trade for what's already mine."

Lilith jabbed a finger to the ceiling. "Was yours. They're in my house now."

The thunder of footsteps raced across the ceiling above them, accompanied by a female shriek. Asher lifted one brow. "You sure?"

Lilith looked to the ceiling, then without returning her gaze to Asher, she raced for the steps. The rapid fire of her heels only punctuated her yapping tone. "If you so much as lay one hand on my girls, Asher, I'll kill you."

"Good luck with that."

"Oh, shut up!"

He strolled to the shelf of cloudy liquid and easy as could be, tucked the bottle under his arm. Sometimes this job came too easy.

He grabbed the hose that serpentined under the prep table and turned it on full-blast. He worked the sprayer back and forth as it pelted Emilia's body with sharp sprays of water. The yellowish film and remaining worms washed away, but Emilia didn't react. Not even a flinch. The girl was teetering on the verge. He couldn't take her though the chaos upstairs. If anyone touched her...it would probably do her in for good.

He lifted her from the puddle of frigid water. The cold soaked into his clothes as he searched for the driest spot possible to hide her. Emilia was a big girl. Despite what Baila knew about her sister, Emilia wasn't a stranger to any of this. Her skills had brought her here. And though he hated to admit it, Gordon could care for her better than anyone. The acquisitions expert could find her aura again, or help her build it back.

Find Gordon. Get him down here. Emilia would be

fine.

Moments later, he found Gordon on the second level, busting down doors with a well-placed kick of his boot.

"I'll call the police." Lilith yelled.

"They're busy. Ran into them on floor one." Gordon slammed his shoulder into the next door with a deafening crack, but this one stuck. He delivered two more savage kicks before the door jumped to half-open and caught again.

Lilith rushed through the gap and spun with her palms out. "Don't you dare. If you take one step inside this room, I'll—"

Asher brushed in front of Gordon. "Allow me." He gave Lilith his most brilliant smile, and yanked the door shut in her face. He turned away from the giggling handle and the thump of Lilith's body against the door.

"Damn you, Asher!"

He frowned at Gordon. "I called the twins, not you. I need you down—"

"Where. Is. She?" Gordon clenched his jaw, only accentuating the schoolboy dimple in his chin.

Asher stepped ahead of Gordon again and turned the next doorknob before Gordon could kick it. The door squealed open and an eerie silence pulled everything to a halt. A skeletal-thin redhead hovered as if in an air-light cocoon, six inches from the bed, her face pinched in soundless agony.

"Not here. Meg's in one-fourteen—" Asher started.

Gordon narrowed his eyes on the embossed door numbers, then turned to the door behind him. "Where's that?"

"Hell if I know. The numbering system in this joint

makes no sense."

"It's done by price," Charlie called from midway up the stairs. He angled his head up. "You're looking for the top floor."

With that, Gordon rushed ahead.

Asher took the stairs two at a time behind him. "Great. Prince Charming here can bust through the sixth floor just in time for their funeral." He glared at Charlie. "What'd you invite him for any way?"

"She's mine isn't she?" Gordon demanded, picking up his pace.

"Emilia?...You're losing your head over that girl."

The men rounded the next level of the staircase. A gathering of Lilith's helpers scattered in a chorus of squeals and swish of colored fringe. Men peered from open doorways in a mix of dread and surprise.

"You're a collector, Gordon. Save the gallantry," Asher continued.

"Since when do I need a lesson from you?" Gordon fired back.

"Since you lost sight on collecting in favor of the smash and grab technique. If you'd done your job, just fucking listen to what I say, we'd be out by now—"

Wood exploded into the hallway of the top floor. As Asher, Gordon and the twins topped the stairs. Asher shielded the bottle he had tucked under his arm. Splinters and dust clouded the image of Harvey cradling Meg as he carried her from room.

Asher spared Gorden a glance. "By the way, Emilia's in the basement."

"The hell!" Gordon shouted.

"Go. Get her out. We'll give you cover." Asher replied.

Harvey met them in the hall. The expression on his face said he aimed to keep Meg for himself, pulling her limp body tight to his chest.

"What are you doing?" Asher warned.

"Finding her a bath, for one. She used to smell like bubblegum, now she smells like a goddamn whore."

He growled just before slamming through the twins' human blockade. "Out of my way."

Chapter Twelve

The humming pain in Baila's head numbed her surroundings. She could feel the presence that sank on the edge of her mattress. The presence that was there...yet wasn't.

It lifted the pillow from her head and shrill breeze brushed over her clammy skin. She wanted to sob. To beg for the presence to give back her feather-down shield. The jazz band had been practicing all day. The rhythmic tap-tap sent shards of pain dancing through her brain, lacerating her nerve endings.

Is this how death would take her, agonizing and slow? With some stupid hippity-hop tune that would never end? That's what her physicians had warned—well not so much the tune, but the rest hit the target. Of course, they also said they'd keep her comfortable, but instead she felt as if she were drifting in an endless ocean. Unable to sink, nothing to hold on to, only flailing pain and fear keeping her afloat.

And why was that?

Oh yeah, because she just had to take that final jump to purgatory. Just had to take all her fortune and toss it to the wind one last time.

Toffee's warmth that had once pressed at her feet pulled away, and he bounded in circles at the foot of the bed. The jostling motion only made matters worse. She curled her feet away.

"Get him out of here," Asher murmured.

Toffee began to grunt and squeal with indignation.

Baila cracked her eyes open, ready to protest. The blinding cloud cleared enough for Baila to see Toffee clamp down on the meat between Asher's thumb and forefinger.

He jerked his hand away and shook it with a muttered curse, then grabbed the bunny by the scruff of the neck. Caught by folds of fur and fat, Toffee swung hammock style back and forth. His legs pumped at a fierce speed, as if daring anyone to get within striking distance. Asher tossed the bunny to...she wasn't sure who, her head hurt too bad to turn it. But the minute Toffee landed, the receiver expelled a grunt. "I'll take him," Liz whispered.

Good. At least someone could care for him after she died. But if someone died in purgatory, where would they go? The tangerine sky didn't look like any window to heaven she'd ever seen. More like some garish Tupperware lid tightly sealed.

The metallic spin of a Mason jar lid rang through the room, followed by a sour smell that reminded Baila of the pickled limes her grandmother used to make.

"Charlie. Clyde, take Liz down to the concession stand. Get all the peppermint sticks you can carry. And don't get caught."

"Who needs friggin' candy at a time like this," Liz said. Her voice grew more agitated. "You're not getting rid of me that easy. The other girls are still out cold. Baila needs me."

"No, she doesn't. Not for this."

"Why? What are you gonna do?"

"Twins—" He snapped. With a scuff of footsteps,

the twins took action.

"The peppermint will help with Baila's headache," Charlie explained.

"Yeah, right. Get your hands off me. I'm serious. You think Toffee's bad, I will totally bite you where it counts."

"That's okay. Charlie here likes the rough stuff. He's been looking for a little nibble for quite some time," Clyde replied. His voice sounded more distant and closer to the doorway.

"Oh, shut up. I have not." Charlie grumbled.

Clyde chuckled with his voice sounding halfway out the door. "Oh, must have been me then."

Their voices died away with the faint click of the door.

She knew she wasn't alone though. Asher had never left the bedside. Even now she could feel the weight of his stare boring into the pillow that covered her head.

"Baila?" He lifted the corner of the pillow. "I need you to take this."

Her stomach clenched at the sour smell tingling her sinuses. "Not meant for human consumption, remember?" She whispered with her eyes still closed.

"This one is." He helped her to an upright position. When he straddled the bed behind her, he blocked any chance to recoil under the covers.

Her face pinched at the first drop that splashed onto her tongue. The fumes overpowered her senses and she lurched forward in a reflexive gag.

Asher held her chin with an iron grip. "You have to take it. All of it."

She managed a few panicked breaths before he

tipped the jar to her lips again. She latched onto his wrist.

The faint stubble of his jaw line grazed her temple and a chilled breath fanned her skin. "Come on you can do this."

Her next struggling gulp left a bitter film behind. She quick-gulped again hoping to down as much as possible before taking another breath. The next swallow chased down more easily, but she had to come up for air. She managed one more half-gulp before seizing a sharp gasp.

She coughed through the searing fumes and fought her lurching stomach to retain the mixture. The remaining strength poured from her body and the world fell dark around her."

****

When Asher laid her back, her abdomen continued to clench and release with enough force to rock her whole body. It looked damn painful. He swallowed hard and brushed a stray tendril from her forehead.

"That's it. Keep it down. Just a little longer," he murmured. But he wouldn't blame her if she barfed all over him. He'd deserve it. Dragging her down here into this misery, he deserved far worse for all the pain he'd caused her—continued to cause her.

Healing her wouldn't change anything, only stave off the inevitable. Sooner or later Baila would die down here. He could delay it, but he couldn't change it.

He pushed out a deep sigh when her convulsions calmed.

The elixir would gradually purify a healthy victim, but this girl was about as sick as they come. Her body would never cleanse completely. The elixir would break

177

up the impurities but it wasn't strong enough to release them all. Baila had just become a contagion.

To leave her like this would be unconscionable. Any unsuspecting local who siphoned her tainted aura would become contaminated. The entire population of purgatory could wipe out in a matter of days. Not even their precious amulets would save them. The cancer would block their ability to retain aura, and they'd all become repeaters.

Asher watched the heavy rise and fall of her chest as he forced a cold breath into her lungs. He pulled back to reveal tiny ice crystals forming on her lips. A wisp of dark mist swirled from her mouth and formed a churning halo high above their heads.

The glow of her aura seemed to darken with each passing second. The cancer swarming through her body must be doing some major damage already. She looked so… depleted. His heart squeezed and he cradled her hand in his. It would be difficult to keep her alive if he didn't hurry.

He forced in one more breath, crushed his lips against hers, and sucked the air back hard.

With the sharp intake of breath, tiny shards of glass seemed to catch in his lungs. The spasms in his chest became uncontrollable. A deep, bone-rattling cough seized him until his throat turned raw and a fine mist of blood sprayed the floor.

When he recovered long enough to wipe the blood from his mouth, he returned to Baila's side. The same black glittery crystals that must have caught in his lungs, were lifting from her mouth like a thousand dandelion seeds caught on the wind.

The process went slow, but he could see it

working. Her aura brightened. After a few moments, she emanated a soft amber glow that seemed brighter than ever before. More brilliant than the first time he'd seen her, before he'd even taken that first sip.

He'd done it. He'd healed her.

Asher used a pull of energy to draw together the churning mass above him until it compacted to a small hill of frozen grains in his hand.

Time was of the essence now. If he didn't find a place for the cancer to go, it would find a way back to her and this time it would be impossible to remove.

He had to find another victim, and fast.

****

Most days after the skin-searing ride through the gateway, Asher could find his bearings pretty quick.

But not today.

When Asher revealed himself, a flurry of color and activity surrounded what was once the predictably docile portal. It appeared to be some hideous combination between fleeting memories of his past and purgatory's present—if you could call it that.

Young women were mashed against the fence like crazed groupies, dressed in clingy gowns of every color. Their faces were frozen, eyes wide and jaws slacked, in a mix of fear and surprise. Some men, the smart ones, the moveable ones, were intent on pulling their frozen friends back.

A handful of police officers, looking about as exasperated as Asher felt, paused mid-way to wedging themselves between the mass of people and the chain link. A futile effort, the crowd already outnumbered them ten to one.

The few youngsters bold enough, or dumb enough,

to have hopped the fence, staggered back, poised to retreat.

The crowd beyond the fence mixed with gasps and murmurs as he approached, only fueling his irritation. It happened every so often, stealing a hometown sweetheart tended to cause a few waves. Stealing four of them apparently caused a well-dressed tsunami.

On a regular day, he'd probably snag the closest victim and head back to the portal again. He didn't really care who. These people needed to learn that the gateway's collectors were equal opportunity abductors. But for the first time, Asher wouldn't be taking his victim. He'd be leaving them here to die.

One portly woman's voice rose above the crowd. "Please! Gadspy, please! Bring her back. Bring her back, or let me take her place."

Maybe it was the shrill quality of her voice that drew him or the uppity thrust of her chest as if she owned the place. He laughed. "Since when has anyone come back?"

She adjusted her stance as if waiting for him to reconsider and stole an asking glance to the mass behind her. Ah, playing it up for the crowd. Nice.

He approached the woman with the mousy brown sausage curls.

"You want to take someone's place, do you?"

"That's right," she replied.

"You really think you're brave enough for that?"

"As brave as they come."

No he'd seen "as brave as they come." Baila was as brave as they come. This woman had merely built herself up on fame and popularity.

When she eyed the skeptical lift of Asher's brow

and a scowl soured her face. "You think I'm afraid of you? I know you, Gadspy."

"Name's not Gadspy. And you don't know me."

"You want what you asked for? Very well then." He opened his hand and blew the puff of dark grains into her face.

She winced, scrubbed at her eyes, and turned her face away. "What was that for?"

"Just giving you what you wanted."

With a jerk from his amulet, he flashed back to purgatory.

Chapter Thirteen

Baila turned in search of any cool spot she could find on her pillow, but there was none. Her eyelids squeezed tighter against the blinding light. Even with them closed, scalding tears ran down her cheeks as if staring into the afternoon sun. Heat flared from her skin and warmed the sheets around her. She kicked at the unbearable tangle of sticky silk.

"She's coming around," one of the twins said. His voice sounded distant, whether from the pool of tears collecting in her ear canals or the foggy effect on her brain, she wasn't sure.

Clipped footsteps approached. *"Coming around,"* Clyde mocked. "As if I couldn't tell. Just look at her. Like a human bug zapper."

The ruffle of silk met her ears before the suffocating fabric covered her body again. She grimaced. "Don't—" Her voice sounded thick and distant.

The twins continued without acknowledging her. "No. A light house is more like it. And if she keeps this up, her aura will bring every repeater in a ten mile radius," Clyde said.

Baila fisted the cloth and flung it away from her body again. What was happening to her? Why couldn't she see? She clawed at the muggy dress that bound her torso and tangled around her thighs. There might be men in the room, but she didn't care who saw her undies at this point. Reaching back for the zipper, her fingers, slick with moisture could only graze the metal. She reached again from under one arm but couldn't pull the zipper more than a few inches.

Off. She had to get it off.

Her knuckles burned as she tugged her left shoulder strap down and tried to yank her arm free. "Asher…" The word tripped over her tongue. He must have done this.

It felt worse than death, worse than hell. Her heart galloped in her chest and her breath felt heavy and constricted.

Clyde's voice drew nearer and a warm mound of silk poured over her head again. "Yeah, well don't you dare get any ideas about going toward *this* light, little brother. Don't need you getting all apple sauced too. With Gordon already balled-up over that blonde one—"

"—you mean Emilia," Charlie corrected.

"—Yeah… yeah and Asher's got his hands full with this—"

"—I believe her name's Baila."

"I don't care about her blasted name! Point is, we've got two of our main guys already preoccupied with skirts and under-thingies, and now…Harvey's disappeared with Meg." The last few words came out more solemn, but Clyde seemed quick to recover. "We can't afford mistakes here. Our jobs, our livelihood is on the line. If someone doesn't right this car and quick, those girls will be slaughtered. Our amulets taken. I mean it, Charlie. We're losing control here."

Baila thrashed left and right as Clyde worked around the bed. He tossed and tucked cloth about as quick as she threw it, as if to make sure no patch of skin met fresh air. She punched and failed, but Clyde only pulled the cloth tighter.

She kicked.

He jerked.

She let go a shriek of frustration, but he continued his task without pause.

Couldn't they hear? Why wouldn't they help her?

"—And to make things worse, we have to drag this one downstairs…Would you stop fighting?" Clyde snapped.

"No!" Baila screamed. At least she hoped it sounded like no. She wasn't sure how much of the sound carried through the cloth. She stretched her arms above her head. When she found the edge of the sheet, she hooked her fingers around it and yanked.

She gasped when air brushed her face, but the breath still felt warm and thick. Baila gave another desperate tug to the shoulder strap of her dress. The seam popped.

"She's gonna rip it," Charlie warned.

"What do you want?" Clyde's hand clamped down on her wrist.

She jerked away at the initial shock of cold steel.

Clyde continued, just as irritated as ever. "She has to face that crowd in a few hours. She can't go naked. We gotta prove nothing bad happened last night, you know? That she's got that healthy glow." Clyde seemed to pause, as if contemplating the stupidity of his own words.

Baila went for the shoulder strap again. Her senses perked with apprehension. She feared the ice would come again, but she couldn't bear the fire any longer.

184

"Oh, she's got a glow all right. Send her down like this and it'll be like lions ripe for the kill. We're going to need more muscle…" Charlie's voice softened. "Do yourself a favor and lift her already. It tends to calm them down."

She yanked one arm from the dress, then the other, and shoved it to her waist. Baila opened her eyes again, but shut them just as quick and guarded against the burning sensation with both palms.

Her stomach clenched as the bed beneath her disappeared and she felt herself floating in midair. The silk sheet that draped her left leg slipped away as Baila struggled to shift the dress over her hips.

"Now don't—"

Her knee collided with something hard and another zap of cold shot up her leg. Her gasp mingled with Clyde's muffled curse.

Charlie snickered from across the room, and it took him a moment to respond. "You okay?"

"Fine." Clyde's voice sounded hollow as if covering his mouth and nose.

"Asher's not going to let this go bad," Charlie said. "He lives by the collector's code, just like the rest of us. Soon as he inflicts someone, he'll be back to right things."

Baila paused. Inflict someone? In all her discomfort, she hadn't recognized the absence of her pestilent, throbbing friend, Tumor. Could Asher really have removed it? And was he giving it to someone else? Her heart felt vised somewhere between hope and dread.

"And in the meantime, Harvey's busy dipping his wick where it doesn't belong," Clyde said.

"You don't know that," Charlie argued.

"Oh, come on! Stop being such a primrose. As if you weren't thinking of doing the same thing? One moment alone, and I know you'd be doing the ol' drill-tap just like I would. We're two halves of a whole, remember? We share the same amulet. We even have to share the same goddamn girl.

"Well, I'll tell you one thing, if our fearless leader doesn't get back soon, I might be tempted to steal Meg back… and take the straitlaced one too."

"Yeah, that's Elizabeth—"

"Would you quit with the names already?" Clyde paused. His voice turned sly. "Waaait a minute. I see that look in your eye. You've got a thing for the straitlace—"

"Elizabeth!" He roared.

"Knew it. I knew there was a dirty smudge somewhere in there. Little brother wants to soil the str—"

"Not going to say it again. Her name is—"

"Elizabeth. I got it." Clyde's voice trailed in thought. "Bull Whip Lizzy." He paused. "Hey, you think she's got a naughty side? Maybe that's why they call her that."

"How should I know?" Charlie spat.

"But you want to find out."

Amid the argument, Baila kicked free from the last folds of her dress. It didn't add much comfort though. More overheated than when she started and with muscles of jelly. Baila could only lay there flaccid, panting, and praying for something—anything to take the heat away.

Clyde and Charlie fell silent as a scuffling sound

entered the room.

"Aren't you supposed to be watching this one?"

Baila didn't need her eyes to recognize Asher's all-taunting tone, but she stiffened when she heard an accompanying yelp from the female that must have entered with him. She sounded young. Did he bring someone new? She cracked her eyes to a bleary vision of three broad pillars of darkness looming near the door. One female frame stood out among them. A soft light flickered around her. Liz.

Charlie sounded surprised. "She's drunk."

"Oh. Na-ugh-ty." Clyde elbowed his brother.

"Shut up," Charlie muttered.

"Her aura's pretty faint from all the wine, but she'll put in an appearance." The broadest of the dark shadows loomed closer. "Good morning, sunshine." The soothing tone of Asher's whisper coupled with a cool touch against her cheek. Not sharp like Clyde's had been, but a wispy sort of cool. She turned to seek it out, but the touch disappeared. She bit her lip and moaned her frustration as she reached out to him. But he pulled away.

Why?

Why! He had done this to her and he can fix it.

"She's still out of her mind,"

"Am not—" she fired back.

Charlie paused. His voice wavered with uncertainty. "Oh-kay, maybe not. Not sure how the hell that's possible. Explains the fight she put up though. How much of that juice you give her anyway?"

Asher's shadowed profile shifted as if rolling up his sleeves. "There should still be some left. Give it to Elizabeth. Just enough to perk her up."

"I'm not drinking that stuff," Liz said.

"You've been drinking everything else in arm's reach. Here." Asher tossed the bottle to the twins. "Bottoms up."

The sound of shuffling footsteps and slapping hands filled the room as Liz tried to fend them off. "Don't you dare…" she warned.

"Liz!" Baila's heart squeezed in her chest and she attempted to row herself closer to the struggling trio. She kicked and flailed but the air around her wouldn't stir. "Don't touch her. Liz, don't take it."

The tail end of Liz's pained squeal ended with a gurgle. Then silence.

"Liz?" Baila strained to see through the bleached haze, but the mingle of darkness and light eclipsed from her view as Asher stepped closer. "Liz!"

"Watch her for the next few hours. If she gets too bright, siphon—"

"Don't mind if I do—" Clyde's interjection ended with a dull thud. "Ow."

Asher sighed. His voice took on a hint of irritation. "Just don't leave any evidence…I'll take care of Baila."

The cool caress of his fingers brushed her hair. She turned, ignoring the delicious chill that swept over her and shoved his hand away. Her skin popped and sizzled where her palm struck him, and with a cry of pain, she cradled her throbbing hand. She hoped it hurt him just as bad as it did her. Or worse.

He let them hurt Liz. Her last friend separated from her. How would she find them all now? Like this? How could she save them if she couldn't even rescue herself?

"Your friend will be fine. I told you. I'm here to help. Love me or hate me for it, but that's what I aim to do," Asher said.

L-word, she mentally snarled. That's not fighting fair—that's cheating.

Frost crawled across her scalp as he laced his fingers deep through her hair and tugged her face toward him. She winced, ready for the first blow to strike.

The unexpected caress of his lips on her eyelids held her motionless. In an instant, her shoulders sank back with relief. The burning vanished. Tears ran in cooling rivulets down her cheeks. Her vision dimmed enough to make out the strong line of his jaw, but his hardened expression never reached his eyes. There was a foreign mix or regret and sincerity she didn't quite expect.

The look disappeared as quickly as it has come. He angled his head. "Can't leave visible frost marks." His voice trailed as he scanned the length of her torso. He reached for the silk sheet. "Be a good girl. Try not to struggle."

She took a shaky breath, but her lungs caught and she arched away from an icy flash that zipped down her back. It seemed to cut through skin and muscle and lodge itself in her spine with a numbing ache that remained long after his touch left her.

"Shhh," he whispered.

She strained to hear him over her own anxious cry as he circled her. Evaluating.

"Easy, doll. You're doing fine." He reached for the silk sheets that piled below her and began twisting them into two long ropes. "Trust me."

She cut him a glare. "Really? Trust you? Weren't you the one who got me into this mess in the first place?"

His hands continued their motions, but his gaze met hers with an equally hard look. "I may have deepened this hell hole you've so willingly jumped into, but I didn't push you."

She glared over her shoulder at him as he tucked the fashioned rope between the bed's mattress and frame, leaving a yard of fabric on either side.

"But you *did* push me. Back at the pier when we first met," she insisted.

"A love tap. On your sweet little ass—"

L-word. Baila's thoughts faltered, but she corrected quickly enough to avoid detection. "Oh, Mr. Memory had a breakthrough." The snarky look she gave him fled to panic when he stepped forward. She felt the chill of his body only inches from hers. Baila tensed and held up both palms.

"My memory is selective. Hands down," he said.

The cool flow of air increased to a tickle over her bare abdomen. Goosebumps raced across her skin.

"Feel that?" His voice sounded huskier than before, and glacier-gray eyes darkened with a knowing look. "Feels good, doesn't it?"

How could it not?

His fingers danced over her abdomen, leaving an icy, pale impression behind. The sound of his breath turned heavy as he traced along the edge of her panties. The cool in his touch began to melt from the heat of her skin and soon his full hand splayed across her belly.

"Warmth radiates from a few key places on the human body." He pushed her down, increasing the pressure until she felt herself sinking back to the remainder of rumpled bed sheets. "They're called pulse points," he continued.

Heat throbbed at her back where she met the cloth, the icy zap from his first touch long forgotten.

"Baila? You listening to me?"

"Not really." She squirmed. "Ugh, make it stop." Her hands seemed to move on their own as she reached for him, but he pulled away.

"Listen." He caught her right ankle with a loop of the fashioned rope, and with a quick tug, he restrained it to the bed.

Her heart rate kicked up. She reached for the knotted silk.

"No—" Asher said in warning. He lassoed her right arm with a second loop of silk and in a matter of seconds that too became pinned.

"Why the restraints?" she demanded.

"Its delicate work and you're too impulsive."

"Since when is being impulsive a bad thing?"

"Have you seen your hand? If you move, touch, grab—anything that pulls aura from a visible location on your skin—"

Baila twisted."Stop fighting and open your ears." He moved for her other leg. "Siphoning aura is the fastest way to cool you down, but if they find out I've done it, they'll take you from me."

An traitorous ache invaded her chest as the scenario played out in Baila's mind. They could do that? The thought of being trapped down here, without him, sliced deep and left a gaping hole.

But why? She'd already lost her friends, and her sister. How could being stuck down here without him …hit so hard?

She nodded in resolve.

"It must be undetectable." He spoke the last word deliberate, and the faint lift of his brow seemed to tug her mind into risky territory.

Baila didn't think her face could get any more lit up, but there it went.

Asher flashed a brilliant smile and continued, seeming satisfied—delighted even—that she understood. "I'll let you up as soon as I'm done. So relax...you might even enjoy it."

"Enjoy it," Baila scoffed. She twisted her body away from him and kicked at the cloth that bound her left leg.

"Most women do." With a flick of his wrist, he lassoed her free ankle and pulled it taught.

With only one fist free, she slammed to the mattress in frustration. "I'm not most women."

A sly grin curved his lips. "Well, that's true...but you're still a woman. Tell you what...give me five minutes of your time. If you don't like it, I'll stop." He held out the last strip of cloth and nodded toward her wrist. "Deal?"

Baila hesitated, caught somewhere between the desperate need for his cooling touch and the curiosity of his promise. She remembered, a little too well, how it felt to have him inside her. But she also remembered what he stole from her in the process.

In her current state, he would only be doing her a favor. A mind-numbing, bone-aching, best-sex-of-her-life favor.

She flashed a glance to the sealed door. *Oh what the hell.* She surrendered her wrist into the cradle of cloth.

Asher said nothing. In the length of two heart

beats, Baila found herself tied spread-eagle to the bed. Nervous energy lit a fire in her veins and the urge to squirm seemed beyond her control. She flexed her arms and legs against her restraints.

The cloth eked out a faint protest but it wouldn't budge.

Her gaze turned to Asher as he rounded the bed to her feet.

His amulet emitted a soft glow that seemed to reach for her even through the material of his shirt.

A look of hunger sparked new life into those glacier-gray eyes.

Baila felt the pangs of excitement stir in her belly. The level of risk in this moment seemed higher than any cliff she'd ever climbed. And she wanted to jump. Bad.

Baila's courage seemed to waver the moment the mattress dipped and springs creaked. Must be those pre-jump jitters. She closed her eyes and forced a soothing breath as the weight of him settled between her thighs.

This was so much easier when she didn't have to face him. The memory of when he took her from behind seemed burned in her brain, but this scenario seemed more potent somehow. More dangerous. Without any way to hide all the crazy things he did to her. Could he detect the rush she felt, knowing she was about to give herself over to purgatory's most dangerous collector? To not only taste his power but to unleash a little of her own.

Bracing himself on his forearms, Asher's breath fanned the soft curve of her neck. Her shoulder lifted on instinct to guard against him and she fought the urge to squirm.

Pause. Time-out.

What little remained of her bravery was about to make a U-turn. Heat be damned, this man had complete power over her in this position and if last time were any indication, things could get pretty uncomfortable pretty fast. What if he took more than she wanted to give?

Her thoughts were chased away by a wave of excitement when he peeled back the lace edge of her bra, and lowered his mouth.

With the faintest lift of his lower lip, a puff of cold vapor curled over her nipple. Goosebumps raced across her skin as both his hands began a chilled caress along the outer edge of her breasts.

Or maybe he would be gentle this time. Gentle could be good for her. Very good. Baila released a soft moan of encouragement.

When his hands slid to the hollow under her arms, the heat left her body with one brutal tug. The remaining flash of cold sent her mind into a whirl of panic. Her eyes flew open. She gasped and jerked against the restraints.

Asher lifted his head from where it poised mere inches from her body. His soft lips appeared brushed with color, and instinctively she knew she'd find warmth there. Like she did in that first kiss. Cold then blistering.

The need to reclaim her warmth felt primal. She bit her lip and arched against him in a feeble plea for his mouth. She didn't get far, but he seemed to recognize the gesture. Asher withdrew his icy touch and his husky voice tickled over her breast. "I'm helping you first, Baila. Five minutes, remember? We can have fun afterward…if that's really what you want."

The potency of his stare seemed to bore into her. "But you already want it, don't you?" He paused as if waiting for her to make eye contact.

Her heart rate kicked up as she cut him a quick glance.

Oh, what a mistake.

The flash of white in his grin seemed to echo in the depths of those glaciers, just before he lowered his lashes and pressed a tingling kiss to the tip of her breast. A soft chuckle feathered over her skin, and his hand began a deliberate course down her torso. Her hips writhed beneath him.

And who gave them permission to start acting on their own? Who told that deeper, thrill-seeking part of her that it could have whatever it wanted? Make her feel alive in such an ironic place as purgatory.

His fingertips traced a slow circle around her belly button. Her stomach muscles tightened, but she managed to keep still. Mostly. His fingers roved lower, then back and forth along the lacy edge of her panties. He slipped the cloth to one side and tipped his head. "Tell me, doll. How do you like to be touched?"

Baila bit her lip and looked again to the door.

"You won't say? Want to show me instead?"

She squeezed her eyes shut. Like that would be any easier?

"Mmmm. Without your direction, this'll be more time consuming than I planned." He expelled a small sigh and shifted his body lower, then pressed a kiss to the crevice of her inner thigh. "Course, I'm sure you'll recall we don't have much concept of time here anyway."

The light massage of his fingertips over the folds of

her vagina spiraled a steady rhythm. As his touch deepened, the ache in her belly grew with each ragged breath, and Baila found it impossible to keep her body in check. Her thighs clenched, her hips rolled. She climbed to the crest of her orgasm with each perfectly measured stroke until Asher leaned down, and a chilled puff of air mingled with the moisture between her thighs. She held her breath for the flash of cold to invade her again. Hoping it would never come.

She recognized a distant shadow of the chill the moment his mouth descended on her, but the pleasure overtook before her brain could register any discomfort. His gaze flicked to her again, and this time she caught and held it. Her shoulders sank back to the mattress and the tension in her thighs fell away, opening herself to him completely. That must have been what he was waiting for. He closed his eyes and his tongue danced over her with growing intensity.

Baila couldn't seem to catch her breath. Her limbs tensed against their silk restraints, and her soft cries turned louder and more desperate as she rode out the waves of her orgasm.

****

It wasn't until the room fell into silence again and her eyes adjusted to the dim room that she found him watching her. His chin resting atop her smooth mound. His brow furrowed in a mix of wonder and concern.

Why did that look pour so much emotion over her?

She opened her mouth to speak, but no words would come. Was there something wrong with her? Maybe she didn't want to know the answer.

"You're glowing."

She frowned. "Tell me something I don't know."

She looked to her right hand and gave a feeble tug against the restraints. "Let me up please."

He pushed out a deep sigh and reached for her leg. "I mean you're *still* glowing."

"Well, the heat's gone—"

He stormed around the bed. His steps seemed to echo the growing frustration in his voice. With a quick tug at each restraint, her bonds fell away. "Heat comes from your aura. I've already taken what I could, but you're still glowing, Why the hell are you still glowing!"

She frowned in exasperation. "I...I don't know. I've never glowed before!" She stretched her freed hand out to inspect the amber light that seemed to pulse from her skin in steady rhythm with her heart. "You must have done something right..."

His chest bounced in a silent snort. "I did a lot of things right and don't you deny it." He paused and circled a finger at her. "And it looks like a little of that heat is returning to your face."

She swallowed hard and her gaze fell to mattress. "I can't believe I'm going to say this...but isn't there anything else we can try?"

He planted both fists on the bed. "Well I don't know, Baila. Is there something else that gets you off better than oral sex?"

Her jaw unhinged in shock. "No!"

"You sure?"

Asher swiped at the sweat that glistened on his brow, then paused.

A rumble of footsteps approached the other side of the door just before it burst open. "Knock-knock."

Asher's eyes narrowed, and his face darkened with

rage. "What the fuck are you doing here?"

Harvey shuffled to a stop. "I—uh…brought Meg back."

"How polite."

He offered a faint shrug. "Not like I could keep her. She's not mine, is she?"

Asher folded his arms in front of his chest. "Nope."

Harvey jerked his head to Baila. "And what about yours?"

"What about her?"

His lips twitched. "Hop to it, Romeo. What are you waiting for? Defile that bright shiny thing." His expression turned bitter as he returned his attention to Asher. "That's what we do, isn't it?"

Asher passed Baila a fleeting glance. "We need a new plan."

"What do you mean?" He shoved a hand toward Baila. "She's right there, screw and siphon already."

Asher's words snarled through curled lips. "I. Can't."

Harvey rocked back in brief silence and searched the floor. His brow furrowed in confusion before his gaze lifted. "You need help? A stand-in? Understudy? Whatever you call it?"

Asher shifted slowly to the right, blocking Baila's view. His legs braced for battle.

"Well, you can't leave her like this," Harvey prompted.

Baila wrapped the cleanest section of bed sheet she could find around her torso and eased away from the mattress in search of her clothing.

The conversation continued around her, but thankfully, she had slipped from the main topic of discussion.

At first, humiliation held her tongue, which was probably a good thing. Wasn't much point defending her virtue after what she'd just done. She couldn't argue her way out of this one, not in her current state of nude.

She kneeled down to peer under the bed. No dress. Baila fished through extra sheets and blankets that had piled on the floor, tossing them one-by-one in quick succession onto the bed. The commotion earned a brief frown from Asher but no dress.

A flicker of movement caught her eye near the ceiling. Her shoulders slumped. Well, that's just great.

The flag of midnight-colored, Dupioni silk taunted her with each lazy rotation of the ceiling fan. She closed her eyes and expelled a breath of frustration before climbing to her feet.

She clutched the sheet to her chest with one hand while she stretched the other above her head. Her ears primed for even the faintest snicker. If either one of them so much as breathed wrong she'd kill them! She jumped and swiped for the cloth but her fingertips only brushed the hem. She spared a quick glance to the doorway conversation before making a second attempt.

"When do you have another shipment going out?" Asher asked.

Harvey seemed to pause for a moment.

Asher's scowled. "Don't toy with me. I've seen the barrels in Lilith's basement." He took a menacing step forward.

Harvey didn't seem fazed as he lifted his brow in challenge. "Those barrels are empty. Lilith shouldn't receive more until tomorrow."

"Make it tonight."

"Why? What are you after? Lilith keeps close tabs on everything that comes and goes from the plant. If anything's missing, she'll know it."

"The portal lies directly between Lilith's boarding house and the textile mill. You're going to deliver us there."

Harvey gave him a long look, and then nodded.

"Assuming you've only been delivering empties to Lilith, why does she need them?" Asher asked.

He shrugged. "Soiled linen. She uses silk worms to break down the cloth. Then the fattened worms are sent back to the mill for processing."

Asher stared, seeming to gauge Harvey's answer.

Baila shot the two a skeptical look. Wouldn't it be easier just to wash them? And speaking of linen. Baila returned her gaze on the sailing cloth. She jumped again and fisted the cloth. She dug her nails in, but with a pop and tear the cloth ripped free again.

If only god have given her a few more inches. Emilia could have spared a few. She didn't need the whole six extra inches.

Course if she were more like Emilia, she wouldn't be in this mess. Her heart twisted in a sickening knot. She wrapped both hands around the bed's iron footboard and pulled backward. Baila was nothing if not resourceful. First get her clothes, then it's back to finding the girls. The metal feet of the bed screeched against the rough wooden floor.

Toffee *thumped* out a warning from beneath the bed.

She leaned under and peered through the sticky layer of cobwebs, but Toffee didn't move.

His whiskers trembled in fear.

She reached for him and whispered, "Hey, peek-a-boo?"

He darted away, and then turned to face his assailant again. His eyes were wide with a what-the-hell-is-wrong-with-you look on his face. Not that she could blame him. With all the noises she had been making just moments before. Probably scared the stuffin' out of him.

The doorway conversation stopped, but this time she didn't look up.

"When can I see my family again?" She pushed with her heels, dragging the bed with a shriek, shriek, shreeeek until the bed stood under the ceiling fan.

Toffee scuttled for a new hiding place as fast as his pudgy legs would carry him.

She could hear the grating irritation in Harvey's voice. "See your family? Haven't you figured it out yet, Baila? You don't get special privileges here. We don't schedule play dates."

Asher spoke in slow contemplation. "Apart from Emilia, I didn't think you girls were related."

She climbed onto the soggy mattress with fists planted on her hips and her legs braced. "They're the closest thing to family I have.

"The self-righteous mother's too busy playing it up with the high school crowd, and Dad's too busy playing with the girlfriend. Those are the real play dates. Don't bother scheduling those." Baila timed the next rotation of the fan and launched for the dress as it soared close to her. She caught the silk and stumbled step-over-step as the fan continued to turn, taking Baila and the dress with it.

Springs creaked, the bed frame rattled, and Baila's

balance pitched over the edge.

She let go of the dress, but too late.

Her landing came in a less-than-graceful, bone-jarring thud. She managed to stay on her feet, but the instinct to save herself must have overridden her modesty because the cloth around her torso slipped free.

She pulled the sheet back into place as quickly as her *cat-like reflexes* could manage, but the damage had been done.

The corner of Asher's mouth turned up in that sexy conceited smirk of his, and his chest bounced in a silent snort before he leaned against the wall and flipped the fan's switch. The soft click seemed to echo through the room. Then the dress whispered to the floor.

Harvey was first to break the silence. "Be ready before the band strikes."

Asher appeared to barely acknowledge Harvey's exit. His smirk shifted to puzzlement. His brow furrowed, and his gaze scanned the floor for answers.

Lilith didn't sound like the conservation type. There wasn't any power in it. Her business at the mill didn't make sense at all. There had to be something else going on beside cloth recycling.

"What are you thinking?" she asked.

"I'm thinking we need salt. And lots of it."

****

The occasional drip echoed off the cement walls of the Saltair's expansive basement. Baila's muscles clenched at the shock of frigid salt water. She crossed her arms around the toga-style sheet that covered her body. Her voice escaped in a tight whisper. "Is this really necessary?"

Asher hovered with his feet only inches above the water. He continued towing her deeper with a hand fisted in the bed sheet surrounding her. "Got to cool you down somehow." Asher grinned over his shoulder, and his attention dipped to her cleavage. "How's the water?"

Baila squeezed tight to block his view and guard against the assault on her painfully tight nipples.

The water climbed up the sheet, rendering it transparent as the chill seeped into her skin.

Baila slowed her pace and shifted her weight from one foot to the other, her baby-steps a feeble attempt to put off the descent into the Saltair's dark swimming pool. Her eyes narrowed to tiny slits as goose bumps raced up her shoulders. "Come in and find out."

Asher said nothing. He offered a challenging lift of his brow and jerked at the knot she had tied at her shoulder.

Baila gasped and grabbed for the sheet. She managed to rescue a few scant inches but watched with her jaw unhinged as the sheet billowed around her, lit by her aura's glow like a Chinese lantern. She pinched and lifted the remnant of dry material, but it what good would it do now? No way would she press the soggy cloth to her body. She relinquished the sheet to its saltwater grave. "You didn't tell me I'd be coming out here to skinny dip."

His lips curved to that predictable grin. "I hadn't really planned it… but I'm not complaining either."

She dealt him an angry frown. "You're a jerk."

"You decided this just now?"

She shoved the water toward him with both hands.

He jumped back to avoid the spray and his grin

only widened.

"Get over here and take your medicine." She splashed harder.

Asher's brows shot up and he held up both hands. "Okay, enough."

But Baila wouldn't be satisfied until every inch of him dripped. She lunged forward to close the distance between them.

"Stop." Asher's word came out more stern than expected.

"Why? You deserve it." She splashed again.

He jerked his hand back and muttered a curse as if he'd been burned. "That might be"—he gave his hand a moment of inspection before brushing it across his shirtfront—"Salt and spirits don't mix."

Baila remembered a passage in Emilia's book about throwing salt over one's shoulder to avoid ghosts. Even her comment at dinner the other night. But wasn't it just a silly superstition? Most of the theories in that book were.

Asher continued with a weary nod. "And now that you've bathed in it no one can touch you. Not even me."

"What?" She lifted her arms and stared at the ripples that seemed to tug the heat from her body. "I can always wash it off."

"Don't even think about it." Asher turned to retrieve a towel. "Besides, it's only temporary until I get you somewhere safe."

Baila was already marching back to the edge of the pool. She rattled off options between each thrashing step. "Are we following Emilia then?"

Asher shook his head. His attention remained on

the towel as if somewhere in the tiny woven strands of fabric, he'd be able to find an explanation. "Your sister is traveling with Gordon, through the most dangerous place in all of purgatory. The Outer. It's infested with hoards of repeaters who would overpower any ghost or human the moment they stepped inside. It's her best shot at seclusion until she heals. No level-minded inhabitant of purgatory would hunt for her there. Emilia's aura is dim enough now that she just might survive"—he offered her the towel—"but there are no guarantees."

"But as far as you're concerned." He gave her a long look.

"Not a chance, huh?"

"Nope."

Baila set her shoulders. "Well then, what are we waiting for? It's not like I have anything left to lose."

He let go a soft chuckle, and his eyes seemed to spark with a mix of admiration and regret. "This thrill ain't worth seeking, doll." He turned to a nearby bench and grabbed a pile of cream colored silk. She hadn't recognized it at first, but as soon as he let the wad unfurl in his hands, a sickening weight dropped to the pit of her stomach. Her prom dress.

"You're getting the easy way out," he announced.

"Wha—"

"—I'm taking you back. Harvey will be delivering you to the gateway. You're going home."

She swallowed hard to retrieve her voice. "But you said it yourself. No one goes back."

"And for good reason. You send enough humans back through the portal, it'll reverse the pull of energy and seal up completely. The good folks of purgatory can't have that, now can they?"

"You're really willing to condemn everyone in purgatory over this? Why would you do that? Have you lost your mind?"

Asher lowered his voice to a somber whisper that her ears could scarcely detect. "We've had our time, Baila. This is your time now."

Baila scrubbed frantically at her skin with the paper-thin towel. Her arms and thighs took on a reddish hue that mixed with her glowing aura. The resulting color began to mirror the everlasting sunset that poured through the basement windows. Maybe if she scrubbed hard enough the brightness would fade. Maybe he would change his mind. "I can't go back looking like this. And my time ran out anyway."

"Most humans back home can't detect it. You'll be fine." He stretched a hand out to offer her the dress while the rest of him maintained a safe distance.

The very sight of his hesitant posture made her throat thick with unshed tears. This wasn't what she wanted. She wanted him. Pressed close to her body, taunting her and teasing her like he always did. This wasn't Asher. This was a different person entirely.

She shrugged away from the offered dress and continued to scrub with both fists. Her skin burned like the back of her eyes as the tears fell into the puddles of cold water at her feet.

"For such a thrill seeker you sure are afraid to live your life." He nodded to her hands. "Pretty sure you're dry now."

"I'm not afraid to live." She scrubbed harder, faster, but it would never go away, would it?

"I said enough…That's enough…Baila, stop!"

"I'm not afraid to live. I just…don't want to leave you."

He frowned and opened his arms for inspection. "I'm a lost cause." But somehow the gesture seemed half-hearted.

"Yeah, that's what they said about me." She stepped forward her heart squeezed in apprehension. But Asher stood still, as if nothing in the world could touch him. His features looked smooth as polished granite. Guess the salt would only hurt him for a moment anyway. Then he'd forget it even happened. Before long he would forget her entirely. And why didn't that seem to bother him?

Baila swallowed to steady her voice. "We might be lost, but we're not impossible."

Asher squeezed his eyes shut and let out an impatient sigh. "If I wanted to let you go, I would have by now. But I couldn't. And now look at you. You're going to die down here."

She drew her brows together in a plea for mercy. "I don't care. I don't want to go." Maybe that sounded more like a spoiled toddler than she intended, but it was true. The words choked in her throat. She inched closer, gauging his reaction for the first hint that he might recoil. "My life was over. I was sick, Asher. I brought myself here."

He spit the words out in a mix of frustration and disbelief. "However destructive or inconsiderate you were with the remnants of your life, I will not pull the final string."

"You say that like it's a bad thing."

"It is, Baila! When you take someone's life it's always a bad thing. Regardless of the circumstances."

"If it's about leaving your girls again—" he started.

"I already said. It's you. Why don't you believe that?" Her gaze dropped to the floor at the words that slipped off her tongue. She searched the gritty concrete for any chance to slurp them back up again.

Nope. Gone. And she couldn't deny them now. Her next lung-aching breath rushed out just as quickly as the last. "Don't you want me?" She couldn't look at him, but God, how she wanted to touch him—to beg his permission to stay. Baila stepped forward again, before her legs could crumple beneath her, and she buried her head in his chest.

Asher lifted his arms. She could feel him staring down at her. This whole outpouring of hormonal sappiness had to come as a surprise. But Baila was nothing if not unpredictable. And that's what he liked about her, right? Or even loved?

Just a little?

"We've played this game before, doll. You seemed to want me then too. The railway? Remember? That first night?"

"That kiss?" she countered.

Asher paused.

Okay, so maybe she had been the quintessential cat to the bathtub their entire relationship, fighting him at every opportunity. But maybe she liked it that way. Maybe she craved the battle he brought to her life, even more than life itself. She couldn't blame him if he thrust her away and called her a self-absorbed, thrill seeking, macabre groupie. She wouldn't blame him, but at the same time she had to at least try to prove him wrong.

Baila's heart warmed when thick fingers laced

through her hair as he cradled her head closer.

His breath tickled over her scalp and he kissed the top of her head. "You don't have a choice. You can't stay, and I can't let you."

One moment on the verge of melting into him, the next, nose first into the concrete wall she called reality. Something inside her heart cracked, and a wave of grief rushed through her. He was letting her go?

"Then come with me." Just when Baila though she couldn't grovel any lower, let's break out the shovel. There had to be another way and she had to find it. This couldn't be the end. Warm tears trickled down her face.

He shifted to one side and tipped his head. "What am I going to do? Hide in your closet every time your mother starts up the stairs?"

"We'll get a place of our own." She lifted her head. "And how do you know about my mother anyway?"

He gave her a flat look. "That was a joke. I can't leave Saltair. Can't materialize without the portal's energy."

Baila pulled back at the tiny hissing sound and the smell of sulfur that curled to her sinuses. Smoke lifted from where the damp ends of Baila's hair grazed Asher's chest. Her mouth dropped open, and she reached for him, but Asher held up his hands. "It's fine. I'm fine."

Baila fought the flow of tears that wavered her vision and set her chin. "I'm not giving up.

I'm not leaving."

"Baila—"

But she didn't want to hear it. She turned back for the stairway. Where to go, she wasn't sure, but it sure as hell wasn't home.

"Not one more step." His words came in a fierce hiss as she gained momentum up the first flight of stairs.

Baila's senses heightened with Asher marching at her back. She quickened her steps with the adrenaline sharp in her spine. Any minute now he could hook her ankle, and face first she'd land on the cold steps.

Wait a minute. He wouldn't do that. With the amount of care he took in sneaking her down to the pools in the first place, he had to know the scuffle would draw too much attention.

Her bare feet slapped the first set of steps as she quickened her pace juuuust to be sure. The ground beneath her turned to marble as she rounded to the next flight.

Her feet slipped and squeaked on the cold surface. She clamped onto the railing and scrambled for traction.

Asher took the stairs two at a time, closing in fast behind.

Baila's throat clenched when a quick look behind revealed determination hardening in Asher's jaw.

She recovered her footing and raced up the next flight. She ducked to avoid Asher's reach as he tried to snag her through the railing.

"Dammit. Stop!"

Uh-uh. A mix of excitement and her own brand of determination spurred her on. With thousands of patrons all waiting to get their hands on her, no way would they let her just walk out. She had an entire army at her disposal.

Her path arced wide when Elliott's lanky frame stepped into her path.

He rocked back against the wall, his eyes wide in shock.

Baila brushed past as he appraised her from head to toe then swallowed. His Adams apple bobbed up and down as he reached out to her. "Wha—hey, wait." The words seemed almost an afterthought before he too began chasing her.

Baila tore her gaze away. The sharp noise behind her made her jump several steps. The sound Elliott made seemed to suck back into his lungs accompanied by a wet thud that sagged down the stairs behind her.

The grip on her stomach eased. Asher had saved her. Again.

How would it feel not to have him waiting under every cliff she jumped from? She needed him in her life. A parachute she never opened, because until this moment she never knew she needed one. How could he make her cut that free?

Elliott's tone wheezed in short bursts as he called up the stairs. "One's headed your way."

When Baila met the main floor her pace slowed. The crowd pushed several feet back, and a constellation of beady, pin-lit eyes turned hungry on her. She spun to Asher as he jogged up the last several steps, but his attention didn't fall on her. It was fixed on the woman strolling out from the center of the crowd.

"You see" Lilith boomed. "Asher can't be trusted. In no time at all the girls go missing, and look who's to blame."

The crowd didn't seem to ingest Lilith's words at all, their attention didn't shift, and expression didn't change. It seemed eerily similar to a pride of lions stalking their prey.

The mayor approached and rounded on Baila. He seemed to ignore the counter steps she took to avoid him "She's a bright one Asher. Brightest I've seen. Well done." He lifted his voice as Baila continued a cautious dance around him. "Why, if we could get even ten—twenty girls of this quality it could save our entire way of life."

Baila's next step landed her at Asher's chest, and he closed on arm around her.

"Sorry, this one's defective."

The crowd questioning murmurs turned to gasps when a waft of smoke and the faint crackle that emanated from Asher's body.

The salt. Baila twisted to escape the steal bands of muscle that closed around her torso. The sharp smell made her stomach churn. She let her weight drop and tried to duck out of his arms, but she couldn't.

She cried out. "No. Please!"

He released her before she could gain her footing, and Baila scrambled to stay on her feet. She stared at Asher, but he refused to meet her gaze. His attention still set on his father.

"I know you like her, son. You want her. But you can't take her out of the equation for the rest of us. That's not how we do things."

"Things change." Asher's voice loomed low and venomous.

"That's right. Share," A vacant voice called from the crowd.

The room filled with a buzz of angry mutterings. There had to be at least two hundred or more of them. A paranormal mob was not a mob to be messed with. With their lifting capability Baila wouldn't stand a chance. They could suspend her midair and tear her to pieces.

"This is our way of life. This town depends on you," the mayor persisted.

Asher's eyes narrowed. "You're not prolonging life here. You're prolonging death."

His father tipped his head in challenge. "You're out of line, son…"

Asher mimicked the same head tilt and topped it with a sarcastic grin. "Never been in line."

The faces surrounding them began to change as the conversation continued. The murmurs escalated and bodies shifted. A collective jealous rage crawled through the crowd as the clearing around Baila synched tighter. Asher and the mayor stepped toe to toe and began screaming on top of each other.

The veins stood out in Asher's neck. "I'm putting an end to this."

"She doesn't belong to you"

"—the hell she doesn't!"

"Ever since your mother left—"

"—She didn't leave, you killed her."

The mayor rocked back, and then a scowl replaced his surprise. "Your mother got exactly what she deserved—"

His last word cut out when Asher's fist crashed into his jaw. The mayor wheeled, and his eyes seemed to lose focus before his knees buckled and he crumpled sideways to the floor.

Asher didn't wait for a response. He grabbed for Baila's arm and clamped down so hard she was afraid he'd snap it in two.

They raced out the large entryway of the dance hall

with a thunder of heavy footsteps behind them. Before Baila's feet could touch the first step skirting the Grand Saltair's exterior, her stomach clenched and she flew through the air with Asher at her side. To any other person it wouldn't feel like a blessing, but the locals hadn't let go of their lifting restrictions in town. But any moment now they'd remember that this in fact was all hell breaking loose.

Sagebrush and swarms of brine flies left streaks in her vision, and her eyes teared from the rate that Asher hurled them toward the gateway. Baila shrieked when a sudden stop pitched her forward.

Asher caught her mid-somersault and straightened her. Baila looked back at the formally dressed stampede rising over the hill.

A cloud of dust and sand lifted up behind them as if the entire world were following the charge. The few outliers lifted themselves up and were flying toward him.

She'd never been this close to the gateway before without it sucking her in. With one outstretched hand, Baila's palm could meet the onyx and copper doors, but she'd never loathed touching them more.

She felt the pull of a million tiny threads beckoning her back to where she belonged.

Asher flashed only a hint of a smile—a mix of triumph and regret, as he reached at the back of his neck. A soft click and his chain loosened. "Tell you what, doll. If you can find your way back when this is over, I'd be happy to keep you. I'll even wait right here for your return."

But she knew it wasn't true. He didn't think she'd ever find her way back. A power as bright as hers would blow the portal on reentry. He said so himself.

Baila opened her mouth to protest, but before she could utter a sound, Asher crushed his lips against hers in a kiss that seemed to brand her very soul. His tongue dove and retreated with fierce demand as if to say, *you will not forget me*.

Baila opened her mouth to take in more of him just as she recognized the warm metal chain as it snaked around her throat.

She paused.

Asher whispered soft against her mouth. "Love you, Bails."

But it was too late stop Asher's whip from dragging her into a pit of sub consciousness.

Chapter Fourteen

The snap of the heavy cloth curtain sparked Baila's awareness.

She jack-knifed upright and into a tangle of tubes and wires.

A gasp tore from her throat.

She leaned back from her upright position and frowned at her surroundings. Then at the blood pressure cuff strapped to her arm.

What happened? Where was she? This couldn't have been a dream.

The physician appeared from around the curtain and gave an apologetic nod, but the greeting didn't remain for long.

Starting forward, his attention seemed already focused on the task at hand. The four-by-four square of gauze that someone had taped to her chest. "Sorry to startle you. I guess I have the first honor of welcoming you back. I'm Doctor O'Ryan."

"Guessed that from your name tag," Baila snapped.

Under normal circumstances, she gave the new clinicians more leeway, but not this time. Purgatory had been real, but now it was gone.

Waking up to four mauve painted walls and the smell of antiseptic made her want to vomit right into his neatly embroidered lab coat pocket. Anger and frustration spilt over into her veins as she squinted at the lettering. "And what does ABPS stand for anyway."

"American Board of Plastic Surgery."

She gave him a flat look. "What, my frequent flier miles finally earned me that pair of free boobs?"

She scrutinized O'Ryan's face, but he gave her no reaction. As though the countless books he fell asleep in during medical school had wiped him clean.

The skin on her chest burned as O'Ryan peeled back the tape at the edge of her wound. "Just want to take a peek at that nasty burn of yours." He tipped his head and peeled the tape back further. "Mmmm. Pretty intricate. How'd you manage that?"

Baila looked away before the urge to slap his hand overtook her. "Haven't you heard? Burning is the new tattoo."

It was obvious he didn't really want to hear her explanation anyway. He shifted to one side and stretched the skin this way and that, as if buried somewhere in there he'd find his own answer. All by his balloon-headed self. "Yeah, well, there's burning, and then there's crispifying."

She lifted one brow. "That a medical term?"

"What's all this hassling the new guy for, Bails?"

Baila didn't have to see the nurse's aide. She recognized his raspy, barrel-chested voice even before the door clamped shut and he cleared the curtain.

She frowned. "I have tenure, Bruno. And he's only a resident. It's my personal obligation to weed out the weak ones."

O'Ryan continued without the faintest change in tone. "She's a feisty one, isn't she?"

Bruno rounded to the other side of the bed and gave his classic smoker's grin. "Always has been."

"Can't help it. This place brings out the brat in me."

Bruno chuckled. That wasn't really his name, but what sort of mother names their son Arles anyway? He needed something big and burly. As a decorated veteran of Guardian Memorial Hospital, and the only one able to stand up to Baila's ever-teen temperament, he'd earned it.

O'Ryan sat back on his swivel chair and gestured toward the wound with his pen. "I'm guessing someone *down there* gave this to you?"

Baila folded her arms. She didn't try to hide her grimace. In fact, she even made it extra snotty.

Just for him. "Down there? As in, like, Australia?"

His brows lifted in that smug, talking-to-a-mental-patient look. "You know exactly what I mean, young lady."

"Well, then, buy a compass, because purgatory isn't down. It's UP!"

Bruno lifted one finger with a grin he didn't even *try* to bite back. "I don't think a compass would help determine up from down."

"Oh, shut up." She pretended to straighten her pillow, then punched it twice for good measure. But no amount of straightening would ever make her comfortable here. Her varying definition of hell seemed to be getting clearer with each passing minute.

"Look. It doesn't matter. It's just a black scar in the sky now anyway. Can we get back to business?" O'Ryan asked.

"What?" The word just sort of slipped out from the numbness that took over her tongue.

"The gateway," Bruno prompted. "It's gone now,

thanks to you. Of course, the area's sealed off and the government's still investigating, but they're pretty sure—"

Baila stared. *No ... no, it couldn't be.*

O'Ryan touched his pen to the paper as if making a tiny check mark. "Well, at least we've established where. Now let's talk about how. Do you remember? We found you out cold nearly nine hours ago."

Baila silently cursed herself for having let even the smallest grain of information slip. She craned her neck for a look at the clipboard, but the physician parried her movement and angled the paper away.

"The best way to undo it, is to figure how it was done in the first place." O'Ryan prodded. "A laser? Hot knife? Maybe a branding iron? I can't imagine acid could be that precise..."

Baila could feel the rush of anger coloring her cheeks. "I don't want to talk about how. Doesn't matter how. The only thing that matters is fixing me. And I'm not broken. So congratulations, Doctor, you've completed yet another assignment. Now if you'll be so kind as to take your little bow and exit stage left. Continue on with your day."

He paused. "You mean you don't want it off."

Finally a reaction. Baila mimed the same raised-brow expression just to prove it. "Whatever gave you that idea?"

"I did." Baila's mother announced as she entered the room. A barrage of camera flashes and muffled voices cut off behind her as the door slammed shut. The purposeful *clip clip* of her heels carried across the floor before she threw the curtain back.

Baila lifted both hands. "Can't you people knock?"

The good doctor's cheeks turned pink with banked annoyance. "I can see you're upset. I'll come back later."

"What time does your shift end again?" Baila called after him. "So I know when I'm good to escape."

Her mother's laughed. "If you wanted to leave, you should have let the man do his job, not chase him away, wasting time and money. This isn't your personal hotel room, you know. Just let him get rid of that thing so you can go home."

She cupped a hand over her chest. "It doesn't hurt. Besides, you're not removing it. This is mine. My—" She paused as her mind whirred to a halt.

Her passport. Her ticket in and out of the gates of purgatory. Baila's thoughts began to cartwheel faster and faster. With the key this close, branded into her very skin, she refused to believe the gateway was gone. She had to see it for herself. And if it were true? Well, she just find another way in. Asher said he would wait for her.

But would he be able to? The doggy paddle of unease in her stomach didn't think so. The locals would never let him get away with what he'd done, no matter how smooth his conviction. Asher was in trouble.

The urge to vault from her hospital bed and make a break for the exit kept needling at her. She wasn't kidding about the shift change. Experience proved when the nurses excused themselves to report to the next oncoming shift, the halls went vacant.

That would be her chance.

****

The sun had set hours ago outside her hospital window, and it didn't seem at all as refreshing as she hoped. It struck fear and uncertainty because tomorrow would be a new day. Another day without Asher. Followed by another and another. She had to get back to him.

Baila kept an uneasy focus on the cameras flashes outside the frosted pane of her hospital door as she slid from the bed. The sheets scraped against her wind-burned skin. She made her way across the room. Her mother's guarding silhouette shown in the pebbled glass as she shifted to one side, then the other.

Baila gripped the handle and flung the door wide. The reporters lifted their attention and a few opened their mouths in pause.

They appeared eager to catch her, but they couldn't seem to get away with her mother's fist clamped on their microphone.

Her mother's back stiffened with awareness, and she hunched over her new scepter like it were the most sought after treasure she'd ever acquired.

Her voice elevated. "When Gadspy first approached me with the proposition I was stunned, but what's a mother to do? You have to sacrifice for your children at all costs."

Baila slid to one side. Her mother followed, as if to shield her from view. Her mother gripped one reporter's sleeve. "As mothers, we all say how we wish we could take the burden for them. How many can say that they *actually* have?"

Baila stepped further when her mother shifted again, but this time the reporter wanded his microphone mere inches from Baila's nose, blocking her exit. "Is this Baila? How do you feel about—"

Bails smacked the microphone away and took off.

Her mother's voice began with that saintly air she'd honed so well over the years. But quickly ran together and lifted to a shrill note behind the rushing crowd. "Catching the cancer so early in its inception was a fortunate thing for me. My chances are great, but it's going to be a long hard road. And you know…it's worth it!"

In an instant, Baila had broken away from the gathering of stunned reporters and raced down the hall.

"Wait! Baila?" a female voice called. It wasn't her mother.

"Hang on. We just want to ask you a few questions!" another voice shouted.

Baila's feet slapped linoleum. Her gaze whirred through the hall, as she identified her surroundings. Third floor. Down the stairs two flights. Into the basement and down the hall. She knew this place like a second home.

There! Stairwell.

She veered right. Slammed into the door's lever, and thrust it open.

A quick glance behind her revealed a galloping hoard of equipment-toting reporters. Camera lights flared and died with frantic strobe light effect as they continued the pursuit.

"Call a code pink!" someone shouted.

Down the hall to the loading dock's neglected side door and she'd be outta here. Baila grinned as she quick-stepped down the first flight of stairs. *You do that. Call a code pink.*

In less than a minute, hospital staff would block off every entrance. No one would be allowed to leave, and she would be long gone.

****

Late summer had warmed the vacant parking lot of the Saltair to the near-scalding point. A thankful change from Baila's hospital-refrigerated state. But although the temperature soothed her, the image of the place left a sickening weight in her chest.

Guess there wasn't too much left to say about the ink-like smudge suspended on the horizon. The reporters had long gone, in search of live mouths with stories to tell. The investigators probably headed home to their families for the night.

For once, Baila felt glad about her mother taking center stage, it allowed Baila all the time she needed to escape. To find another entrance to purgatory.

On the night of the séance, Emilia had mentioned a portal. One so big, she couldn't close it on her own. If the Saltair truly had burned down, not once, but twice, could that portal be another way in?

The weighted double doors of the Saltair's replica swung free, its chains grating along the pavement. The pad of her bare feet echoed faint through the hall.

She used her foot to brush aside the forgotten, fuchsia-colored, crape paper that snaked through her path. Overturned chairs, empty plastic cups and straw wrappers—she'd never seen the place so trashed.

Perhaps Saltair had been left as-is for the cameras. To play up the drama of a prom night gone bad. Or the caretaker has been a little too busy. Mildred—the ghost who kept this place in order—she'd be pissed if she saw it.

Baila rounded the long hallway into the ballroom and cast her gaze to the grayed chandelier. That's where the moths had landed. The portal had to be near there, somewhere.

And where was Mildred, anyway?

She closed her eyes and opened her mind to call out to the caretaker. Baila tried to picture the well-rounded woman with the bright, flowing coat of colored silk. Her shoulder-length, dark curls and olive complexion. The way she seemed somehow more youthful than she let on. And her strange affiliation for necklaces—

Ohmuhgod.

She couldn't call Mildred. No one could. Because that wasn't her name. It was Lilith.

Lilith!

"Can't say it's a pleasure seeing you here."

Baila recognized the malice in her voice long before Lilith took form in front of her. Through a cloud of chilled smoke, her body faded into view.

"Why did you call me?" Lilith demanded. She threw back her billowing scarf coat, fanning away the remaining wisps of smoke. She tore at the Velcro supporting her ample breast pads. The sound split through air, cutting Lilith's rant into short bursts. "What?"—rriiiip—"You want another shot at purgatory?"—riiip rip—"Think you're big, hot boyfriend needs saving?" Her breast pads hit the floor with a thud, followed by a second thud from her butt pads.

Baila tried to stave off the rush of adrenaline racing through her veins. She didn't trust Lilith, and didn't want to let on she had even a vague idea of where the portal *might be*. She had to keep Lilith talking. Just long enough to find its exact location.

Baila edged toward the stairway. "So now that the

gig's up, where's your shortcut? You said you had one. Another portal? Emilia said that ghosts don't know the difference between this replica and the real thing. And I think she saw another entrance here."

Lilith planted one fist on her hip and blocked Baila's path. "Look who thinks she knows so much."

Baila pretended to pan the walls. "Not everything. I don't know why you have the collectors doing your dirty work. You're obviously not squeamish about doing it yourself." She tried twisting a small, candle-shaped, light fixture near the stairway's entrance.

Lilith snorted. "This isn't Scooby-Doo, you know."

Baila didn't respond. She meandered closer to the staircase, and thankfully. Lilith stepped aside. She seemed content that Baila had absolutely no idea what she was doing. Which was mostly true.

"So why are you here then?" Baila prodded. "I can't imagine housekeeping would keep you from your final resting place."

Lilith curled her fingers inward, inspecting her liquored nails. "To acquire the kind of power to run purgatory, I need a few pretties of my own."

Baila started up the stairs, trying to sound even and unrushed. "So besides the girls at your doll house—"

Lilith teetered her head. "—Pretty little toys for the public."

"And the boys at the mill…"

She stopped teetering. "—How do you know about those?"

"On top of all that," Baila continued. "You're taking *even more* people? Sneaking them into purgatory through some secret back door and killing them just for their amulets?"

225

"That's an awfully big assumption." A slow smile spread across her face. "It's a man's world. A woman's got to get ahead somehow."

"Mmmm." Baila nodded to herself.

From the corner of Baila's eye, she caught Lilith's bristling posture as she started up the steps.

"But we're not here to talk about me. You want back in, you know it's going to cost you." Lilith seemed to catch the faint jiggle of her false nose, because her eyes crossed for a moment before she tore it away. "And cake ain't gonna cut it this time."

"I'm sure, but I'm afraid I won't go over well at the Doll House." She scrunched her nose in mock sympathy. "I don't play well with others." She took another step. "And I don't have a necklace—"

"Yes, you do."

Baila glanced to where her bandage crept over the neckline of her hospital gown."Well, that one's not removable." Baila eyed the cage of glass pendants suspended from the ceiling.

Lilith's tone turned menacing-sweet. "But that's not your permanent one, dummy. You get another one…"

"When you die." The last word squeaked with delight just before Lilith vanished.

Baila scanned the room below, but she had to keep moving. She'd have to find the portal on her own before Lilith could stop her.

Lilith's high-noted laughter bounded through the room.

Unease laced up Baila's spine.

Some unseen force gave Baila a brutal shove to the outside edge of the spiral staircase.

She gripped the railing as her upper body pitched forward.

Her chest constricted. Lungs suspended in a painful grip.

She forced herself back in balance.

The pressure retreated, and then prodded her again as she attempted another step up the staircase.

"No. Not that way. The portal's down there. Hurry. Jump or you'll miss it." Lilith's toyed.

Baila knew she was on the right path. But where exactly? Lilith was probably right on some level, She'd have to jump to reach it. But if she missed, even by inches, she could fall to her death. With no guarantee she'd be sucked away to purgatory. If only she had a friendly on the other side to show her the way.

Or a furry…

Toffee!

Baila shut her eyes again, trying to conjure up her old friend.

Toffee, peek-a-boo… Peek-a-boo…Toffee… please.

Lilith's voice took an uncertain turn. "What are you doing?"

Something jarred the glass fixture. Two glass pendants slipped, crashed, and skated across the dance floor.

Baila caught sight of a chunky white tail that was there one second and gone the next. It appeared just to the left of the chandelier about three feet below.

Peek-a-boo, baby, peek-a-boo.

"You're kidding, right?" Lilith said.

There! The rabbit lunged forward again—midair— and just as quick, turned and disappeared from the opening.

Baila raced back, away from the railing. She tried to make her runway as long as possible while she prepared herself for—crazy as it sounded—the leap of her life.

In a blink, Lilith appeared in front of her. The woman adjusted her stance and lifted one brow in challenge. "Going somewhere?"

"Yep." Baila wasn't sure if the nod was for her or Lilith. Probably both. She shoved Lilith aside, sending the woman stumbling.

Now was her chance.

She took one leaping stride, then another. Her heart rate increased the closer she came to the stairway's wide banister. She'd kick off from there and sail into the portal. She could do this. She could…

Baila's hospital gown pulled tight. It seemed to cut into her skin as Lilith tugged her back.

So close… she could still make it.

Baila pushed forward, planting her foot on the banister. Her stomach clenched and she leapt. Arms and legs flailing, Baila fought for precious inches to reach the portal. Its pull tugged her closer. It beckoned her.

Pain shot through her socket when Lilith hooked her right arm above the elbow and yanked her through the air.

Down, she was going down!

Baila cart wheeled through the air. Her gaze flashed to the rapidly approaching dancehall floor.

No, please no!

Before Baila could process what was happening, a numb ache shot up her spine. Her full body seemed to whiplash as she flashed feet-first into the portal.

Chapter Fifteen

All she knew was pain.

Her surroundings had gone black. Tiny sparks of light flashed in her vision.

She had to find release from the bulbous, throbbing joints that were once her knees. She must have landed on them. Baila writhed from one side to the other on the cold floor.

And her back. She tried to stretch. The links in her spine seemed to grate against one another.

A lightning strike of pain began at her neck and ended with nearly losing her lunch. Baila groaned. *Oh, god. Not a good idea. Let's not move like that again.*

She worked to calm her anxious breathing and take in her surroundings. A flurry of mixed music came from all around her, yet it seemed dampened somehow. Distant. As far as she could tell, she was alone. In a room shut off from the source of the sound. She waited for one sound to stand out from the rest. Something closer. But nothing came.

She scooted herself backward to explore the dark world around her. Her bottom scraped against the rough floor. She readjusted the hospital gown that had lifted to her waist, but the cold continued to filter through the thin material.

Baila had a vague recollection of it being wrapped around her shoulders as she flew, feet-first, though the

229

portal.

Another scoot backwards and her elbow bumped something hard. It made a hollow, metal drum-like sound.

She reached out to the ribbed column and blinked hard a few times in an effort to recall her vision. A faint glow of light shown from the cracks in the rafters above her.

The next instant, a brilliant light snapped on. The bulb charged and hummed for a moment as it swung back and forth on its cord.

"Oh good. You're up." Baila recognized Lilith's voice, but failed to locate her through the army of blue barrels towering around her.

Then Lilith was there, pulling her to her feet. The brightness in the room dimmed to manageable and Lilith's sneer of irritation came into focus. "Congratulations. You made the trip just in time."

Baila pulled away but felt hesitant to trust the boggy feeling in her knees.

Lilith hooked her elbow. A cold chill zapped through Baila's arm. "No, this way, this way, silly bird. The crowd is waiting."

Baila stumbled each agonizing wooden step. The music grew louder and more confusing. It seem to energize Lilith, because she became more antsy about making the trip up the stairs. She made tiny bouncing movements on the stair behind Baila. She stepped on Baila's heel. Shoved her forward. "No dawdling," she sang.

The urge to fling her elbow back into Lilith's face became more tempting the further they went. She already had a spare nose, and the hag, plastic one suited her better anyway.

Another cold zap prodded her between the shoulder blades and stole her breath. "Come on. Move it."

Baila shuffled through the polished kitchen toward the screen door. Her stomach churned sour at the sight of them all.

A crowd that seemed so large, it bled into the misty dead-land beyond the boundary of Saltair. The Outer, Asher had called it. The locals didn't seem comfortable there either. They looked...jumpy. In fact, Baila had never seen them more animated.

They looked to one another, and stole fearful glances behind themselves, some even wrung their hands and shifted from one foot to the other. They looked eager to get this over with and escape The Outer as quickly as possible.

The shriek of the screen door muted their uneasy whispers.

As she panned the semi-circled crowd, her attention pulled straight to Asher.

Tied to a single blackened tree in the middle of the yard. His head bent over his chest. Asher's legs no longer supported his weight. He hung there. His arms pinned together in front of him and his torso secured to the tree with a thick, golden rope. A rope that looked all too familiar.

Baila stepped forward, and thankfully, no one motioned to stop her. She hobbled down the steps on aching limbs and over uneven ground to reach him. All attention fell on her, but she didn't care.

"Asher." She cradled his face between her palms. His head felt warm, but heavier than expected. Dread consumed her. She leveled his face to hers. "My god.

231

What did you do? What did you do?"

He couldn't be gone. He was right here in front of her. How could he die? He was already dead. "Asher, wake up." This had to be the same power he had used on her friends.

His head slumped forward again as Baila reached for the rope that bound him.

The swish of Lilith's dress approached Baila from behind. "She's right, Asher. Time to get up." Lilith snapped her fingers and the rope regained its woven-fiber appearance, but it didn't release him. It snaked tighter. Asher expelled a soft moan and a grimace marred his face. He lifted his head and silver, glaring eyes stared into Lilith.

Baila touched his shoulder, hesitant to distract him. The anger radiating from Asher could rival the devil himself. Baila didn't want any of that on her.

Lilith appeared to ignore him. "According to the law and the collector's code, young Asher, purgatory's visionary and only prodigy has executed a criminal act." Lilith sauntered around the tree. "He has destroyed our gateway and nearly destroyed the existence of every person here. For that, he should be punished."

"What about the secret gateway. The one that you've been hiding? Maybe that's why Asher acted the way he did." Baila countered. "Maybe he knew about it."

She searched the crowd for any sign of the other collectors. There had to be someone who could speak for Asher. Someone to argue the charges against him. Baila couldn't find one familiar face in the crowd.

Except him.

Alex. The mayor stared at Baila. A sickening glint

of hunger lit his eyes. He swallowed.

Baila looked away. No help there.

"We're only fortunate that we *did* have a secret gateway, stored for such an emergency." Lilith waved Baila away. "In any event, Asher's fate has already been decided. So let's just cut to the formalities and begin the game, shall we?" Lilith lifted her palms in offering to the crowd.

The gathering of people hummed to life, and Lilith elevated her voice over them. "Now because we've managed to intercept Asher's little collaborator as well, she too will be punished. These two will be taught to share, and share alike." Lilith paused for effect. "Because that's what we do down here."

The crowd erupted in a cheer and edged forward with excitement. Looking from one end of the yard to the other, Baila wasn't sure which way to turn.

Lilith's claws dug into Asher's jaw and she came nose-to-nose with him. "Who's it going to be first, Asher? You, or her?" Lilith's attention fell to his lips and she paused. "Oh, what am I saying? You don't get a choice—" She pushed her lips against his.

Asher's lips twisted in disgust. His shoulders arched in pain and pale discoloration branched from his lips. Frost climbed up his cheeks and chased along his temple.

Baila charged forward and tried to shove herself between them. "Get off him. Get off!"

Lilith fought with her free hand, batting and pushing while trying to maintain her hold on Asher's lips.

Baila went for her face. She shoved, but a large hand shackled her wrist and pulled her away.

Asher?

Her mouth unhinged in disbelief. She looked down to the hand that held her and back to Asher. How could that hand belong to him? How could he want that? Why wouldn't he want her to stop it? She stared.

Why didn't he fight back? Baila's willpower crumbled. Her shoulders slumped.

When Lilith pulled away, she used her fingertips to dab at the edges of her mouth. She met Alex with a smug look of satisfaction when he strode into the clearing.

A tight, political grin pasted on Alex's face. His attention never fell to his son. He cupped a hand on Lilith's shoulder. Lilith wrapped her arms around him, and soon he appeared to be siphoning the aura from Lilith. The very aura she'd stolen from Asher.

Share and share alike. Those were Lilith's words. And that's what they planned to do. Until there was nothing left to share.

Asher's grip on Baila tightened, and he urged her closer. His right shoulder lifted and his second arm emerged from the cord. Baila flicked her gaze to Lilith. Perhaps her distraction was what caused the rope to loosen. Could Asher escape?

But the tension on her arm only increased. It grew insistent. He lifted his head and tugged her tight to his chest. He wasn't trying to get away. What was wrong with him?

No. Baila didn't want any part of this. If they wanted to kill her, fine but she wouldn't be used like this. Not by Asher.

His arms slipped away from her in exhaustion. He leaned in and pressed his forehead to hers. She expected to meet a ravenous monster when Asher opened his eyes. She didn't. They were the same pair of glacier-grays that they had always been. And they were begging her.

"This is the only way out," he whispered. His voice strained. He pressed his lips to hers, gentle this time, imploring.

Baila only felt the pull for a moment before her heart began to hammer in her chest and she jerked away. She shook her head.

He looked down, and then plead again through a fringe of dark lashes. "You're a contagion here. The only way to get rid of them is to use your cancer."

"I don't know what you mean. It's gone." Her words choked.

"Not all of it." Those last words hushed out quick as Lilith approached. Asher continued to stare into Baila as if waiting for her to piece his words together.

Lilith pressed a fist under her nose and expelled a single cough as she turned back to the clearing. Her attention pinned on Asher. "Times up."

"Wait. He didn't get enough—" Baila began.

But Lilith had already latched onto him.

Asher forced his palm between them and tried to shove at her chest, but his arm appeared to flop away in bone-melted surrender. He didn't have the strength left to fend her off now, even if he wanted to. His chest made tiny jumps and spasms as he fought for breath until there was nothing left to give. Still, Lilith didn't stop draining him. She wanted every last morsel.

Baila tore at Lilith again, and this time she shoved Lilith to the ground hard. Her head jostled atop her slender neck, and her initial shock blinked to murder.

"Someone hold her," she shrieked and climbed to her feet.

"I've got her," Alex said. He pulled away from some random woman he'd been sharing aura with—nearly jumped from her arms—to get back into the clearing. He fisted Baila's gown with one hand.

She twisted to retreat.

Alex held his grip, but he turned and broke into a coughing fit that doubled him over. His free hand began searching through his pocket until he pulled out a small, silk, handkerchief.

"Wait. Waaaait!" Elliott, the limber man that once guarded the gateway, bobbed through the crowd. "There's something wrong with her. Can't you smell it?" He stumbled forward, glance back to the unfortunate locals he'd trampled with fleeting apology, and then moved forward again. *"Frosted orchids—"*

Baila wrenched free, and this time, no one stopped her when she raced to Asher's side.

Alex erected his posture, but his shoulders hunched forward once, twice. He looked to Elliott with pause and appeared to fight back the impending cough for a moment, but the cough won out. Alex sprayed a fine mist of blood and black particulate through the air before he managed to cover his mouth with his handkerchief. He stared at the blood-spattered rag in disbelief.

His attention, finally, rounded to Asher. "You've doomed us all," he seethed.

"No, just you two," Baila replied. "And anyone else who dares touch you."

The crowd erupted in confusion and turmoil. Shouts of indistinguishable outrage lifted through the mass of shifting bodies.

Asher didn't respond. His olive complexion had paled to near transparent. His eyes pinched closed. A frown of agony turned down his ruby, grease-smeared mouth.

Baila palmed both sides of his temples. Her nose grazed along his. The warmth in his skin had been leached completely. Chilled smoke wafted from his parted lips. "Asher," she whispered.

Her mouth grazed his when she spoke.

She prayed that Asher would recognize the warmth of her breath. That he would take it somehow.

It wasn't working.

The smell of Lilith's rank perfume had permeated him. Baila didn't care. She meshed her mouth to his and forced her breath in. *Please. Take it, please.*

His cheeks puffed, and the air rushed out again the moment she pulled away.

Baila gripped his hair and pushed his head back, she held his nose, and forced in another lung-aching breath.

Asher's chest tensed. His mouth widened like a baby bird hungry for sustenance. His arms clamped around her and Baila sucked in a startled gasp.

Then he pulled.

That bone-freezing shock of cold chased up her skull and down the back of her legs, until her feet went numb. Pins and needles danced in her joints.

Her body hit the unforgiving ground. She tried to open her eyes, but and Baila lost the strength to lift her eyelids. She could feel her world tip and spin, even after she'd separated from him.

She wasn't sure how much time had gone by in her

battle for warmth. Seeking out the faintest hint of heat within her core, only to have it evade her.

She fought the constant undercurrent of cold that would flood out any spark her body tried to ignite. The shivering seemed to wring every ounce of energy from her muscles.

Then something returned to her.

A voice—Asher's voice—echoed through her head. It sounded raspy, but warm.

That heat flowed along her skin and embraced her body as he lifted her from the ground. "That's some kiss you got there. The kind worth remembering."

Chapter Sixteen

His warm baritone stirred Baila's awareness from its suspended state. "You know, for a place that never sleeps, you sure do get your beauty rest."

She smiled. "Jealous?" Her voice sounded thick and heavy to her own ears. She pulled in a lung-stretching breath.

His tone perked. "That depends. What were you dreaming about?"

She didn't want to open her eyes. Not yet. They still needed to adjust to the bright glow that filtered through her lids. "You, actually."

His fingers smoothed the hair from her brow and tucked it behind her ear. "Why bother when the real thing is lying naked next to you?"

She popped her lids open, and then blinked at Asher's lanterned profile through the golden haze of her aura. She frowned. "You are not."

He grinned and folded one arm behind his head. "But I could be."

Baila shifted. The muscles in her legs burned in protest as she stretched. Her joints ached with thick bands of unyielding tension.

Baila's mouth hinged open in pain. She looked to the rumpled sheet, afraid of what she might find under them. Her knees felt swollen to twice their size.

"Here," he murmured. "Let me." He stood and his

image faded in the dark room then returned at the foot of the bed. A shadow lit only by the glow of her body. "You injured yourself coming through the portal."

"I remember that—"

"—and after I siphoned your aura, you kind of blacked out." Asher folded back the sheets.

"Yeah—" She peered over the pile of silk to where someone had packed her legs with clear plastic baggies filled half-way with water. Wide smudges of purple and blue darkened the honey glow around her knees.

Asher slipped a hand under her right leg and cradled it as he pulled out one baggie at a time and tossed them to a nearby garbage can. "I've been icing you, but you're hot little body doesn't stay iced long." He moved to the other leg. "I don't know if it's helped much." He tossed the final baggie. Asher's attention traced over the mound of plastic bubbles heaped to overflowing in the metal can. Some had deflated, their contents long evaporated. He rubbed the back of his neck. "I forgot how long this takes…" He sighed and pulled the sheets back into place.

Asher rounded the bed to her side again. His attention fell to the sheet covering her chest. With a tender brush of his fingertips, he smoothed the sheet's creased edge. "Thank you, by the way. For helping me. And I don't say those words often so know that I mean it."

She stared at him. What could she say? "You're welcome" didn't seem appropriate. She acted on instinct—and not only because his soul was in torment, but because she loved him.

That's right. The big L-word.

His gaze remained fixed on the sheet, and his brow

furrowed. "And about your mother. Had I known—"

Baila widened her eyes in innocence. "Oh, don't apologize for that—"

His jaw line hardened. "I'm not. I use the word 'sorry' even less frequently. But I do feel sad for you. Because you won't be seeing her again. Not if I have anything to say about it."

Baila nodded in understanding, then paused. "What about my sister. My friends."

Asher eased back onto the bed. "The two barrels sent through the portal on the night of your return weren't light enough to be empty. You should see the mighty tantrum that caused. Meg would be proud."

"And Emilia?"

"She's in a secluded area that skirts The Outer, but she's on the mend. We considered her skills. She's been given the option to return to Earth, and I assume she'll take it. She's agreed to work with Gordon on imports from that end. 'Occult immigration' he calls it. Willing mortals will come and go freely in exchange for donating their aura."

Baila swallowed to steady her voice. She didn't want to ask—not after their last argument. She didn't think she could accept his rejection a second time, but she had to know. Her voice escaped on a breath. "And me?"

"But I want more than your aura. I suppose, you have that same option." His tone lowered to a seductive growl. He leveled his gaze on her. "Lilith and Alex are gone. You've given us a new license here. Another chance to find some shred of normalcy. It wouldn't be fair if I didn't offer you the same."

She tried to look away, but he steered her back

with a gentle nudge under her chin. "I will say, I never should have pushed you away to begin with. It wasn't what either of us wanted. And I'm sorry."

Sorry?

He flashed a teeth-gritting smile. "I just used that word, didn't I?"

Baila's bubble of laughter broke the levee of tears that brimmed her vision.

Asher used the pad of his thumb to brush a lone tear as it raced down her cheek. He pressed a cool kiss to her forehead. "We'll take it one day, one hour, one minute at a time if we have to. And we're going to have a hell of a good time doing it."

Baila tipped her head. "You do remember there's no *concept* of time here, right?"

Asher drew in close. The cool touch of his lips played on hers with each word. "Mmmm. How could I forget?"

A word about the author...

Kacey Mark is a voracious reader and paranormal romance author who makes her home near the Wasatch Mountain range of northern Utah. She loves writing eccentric characters and unpredictable plot turns.

She enjoys a good book that pulls her into its world and holds her captive until the very last page. But then again, who doesn't love that? She's often caught laughing at a book in the middle of a crowded room, and loves it when people wonder what she's up to.

She posts blogs weekly at
http://kaceymark.blogspot.com/
You can catch her on
Twitter @Kacey_Mark
Facebook:
http://www.facebook.com/?sk=pages#!/pages/Kacey-Mark/218199808200456
http://www.kaceymark.com